Agatha Christie

Murder on the Orient Express

Collins

Collins

HarperCollins Publishers
The News Building
1 London Bridge Street
London SE1 9GF

www.collinselt.com

This *Collins English Readers* edition first published by HarperCollins Publishers 2017.

10 9 8 7 6 5 4 3 2

First published in Great Britain by Collins 1934

ISBN: 978-0-00-824967-0

A catalogue record for this book is available from the British Library.

Cover design © HarperCollins*Publishers* Ltd/Agatha Christie Ltd 2017

Typeset by Davidson Publishing Solutions, Glasgow

Printed and bound by Martins the Printers, Berwick upon Tweed

Contents

◆ Introduction ◆

About Collins English Readers

Collins English Readers have been created for readers worldwide whose first language is not English. The stories are carefully graded to ensure that you, the reader, will both enjoy and benefit from your reading experience.

Words which are above the required reading level are underlined the first time they appear in a story. All underlined words are defined in the **Glossary** at the back of the book. Books at levels 1 and 2 take their definitions from the *Collins COBUILD Essential English Dictionary*, and books at levels 3 and above from the *Collins COBUILD Advanced English Dictionary*. Where appropriate, definitions are simplified for level and context.

Alongside the glossary, a **Character list** is provided to help the reader identify who is who, and how they are connected to each other. **Cultural notes** explain historical, cultural and other references. **Maps and diagrams** are provided where appropriate. A **downloadable recording** is also available of the full story. To access the audio, go to www.collinselt.com/eltreadersaudio. The password is the third word on page 6 of this book.

To support both teachers and learners, additional materials are available online at www.collinselt.com/readers. These include a **Plot synopsis** and **classroom activities** (both for teachers), **Student activities**, a **level checker** and much more.

About Agatha Christie

Agatha Christie (1890–1976) is known throughout the world as the Queen of Crime. She is the most widely published and translated author of all time and in any language; only the Bible and Shakespeare have sold more copies.

Agatha Christie's first novel was published in 1920. It featured Hercule Poirot, the Belgian detective who has become the most popular detective in crime fiction since Sherlock Holmes.

Collins has published Agatha Christie since 1926.

The Grading Scheme

The Collins COBUILD Grading Scheme has been created using the most up-to-date language usage information available today. Each level is guided by a comprehensive grammar and vocabulary framework, ensuring that the series will perfectly match readers' abilities.

		CEF band	Pages	Word count	Headwords
Level 1	elementary	A2	64	5,000–8,000	approx. 700
Level 2	pre-intermediate	A2–B1	80	8,000–11,000	approx. 900
Level 3	intermediate	B1	96	11,000–20,000	approx. 1,300
Level 4	upper-intermediate	B2	112-128	15,000–26,000	approx. 1,700
Level 5	upper-intermediate+	B2+	128+	22,000–30,000	approx. 2,200
Level 6	advanced	C1	144+	28,000+	2,500+
Level 7	advanced+	C2	160+	*varied*	*varied*

For more information on the Collins COBUILD Grading Scheme go to www.collinselt.com/readers/gradingscheme.

CHAPTER I

It was five o'clock on a winter morning in Syria. Beside the platform at Aleppo was the Taurus Express[1]. By the sleeping carriage stood a French lieutenant, and next to him a man wearing so many clothes that nothing could be seen but the end of his pink nose and the two points of his moustache.

It was freezing, and both men were shaking with cold. Lieutenant Dubosc did not know why the other man, a Belgian, had come to Aleppo from England, except that it involved a very important job for the French Army. Everything had gone well and now the stranger, Monsieur Poirot, was leaving.

'Let's hope your train will not be stopped by snow!' Lieutenant Dubosc said.

'Does that happen?'

'Not yet this year.'

'Let us hope, then,' said Poirot. 'Are the weather reports from Europe bad?'

'Very bad. There's a lot of snow in the Balkans.'

The conductor appeared a little further down the platform. 'It's time to leave, Monsieur,' he called.

Poirot climbed into his carriage. Lieutenant Dubosc waved goodbye, and the train moved slowly forward.

♦ ◆ ♦

'*Voila, Monsieur*! Here you are!' The conductor showed Poirot to his sleeping compartment.

Hercule Poirot placed money in his hand.

'Thank you, Monsieur.'

'There are not many people travelling, I suppose?' asked Poirot.

'No, Monsieur. I have only two other passengers – both English. A <u>colonel</u> travelling from India and a young lady from Baghdad.'

There were still two hours before sunrise so Poirot took a seat and fell asleep. He woke at 9.30 am and went for coffee. In the restaurant carriage was the young English lady. Tall, slim and dark-haired with cool grey eyes, she looked very efficient.

Soon, another person entered; a tall, thin man of between forty and fifty.

He <u>bowed</u>. 'Morning, Miss Debenham.'

'Good morning, Colonel Arbuthnot.'

The Colonel stood with a hand on the chair opposite her.

'Do you mind?' he asked.

'Of course not. Sit down.'

Like many English people, the Colonel and Miss Debenham did not talk much at breakfast. Soon Miss Debenham went back to her compartment.

At lunch the two again shared a table and their conversation was more lively. Colonel Arbuthnot talked about India and asked Miss Debenham about Baghdad, where she had been a <u>governess</u>.

Later, as they passed through the magnificent scenery of the Taurus mountains in southern Turkey, the Colonel and Miss Debenham stood together in the corridor. Miss Debenham <u>sighed</u>. Poirot was standing near them and heard her say:

'It's so beautiful! I wish I could enjoy it!'

'I don't want you to be involved in all this,' replied Arbuthnot.

'Sssh, please. Sssh.'

'Oh!' Arbuthnot glanced at Poirot with an annoyed look. 'But I don't like the idea of you as a governess – with those awful mothers and their children telling you what to do.'

She laughed with a laugh that sounded just a little mad, and they said no more.

'Strange,' thought Poirot.

They arrived at the city of Konya in central Turkey at half past eleven that night. The English travellers got out to have a short walk.

Poirot, too, stepped down to the busy platform and began to walk along it.

Soon he saw his companions standing in the shadow of the train. Arbuthnot was speaking.

'Mary—'

The girl interrupted him.

'Not now. When it's all over – *then…*'

Politely, Poirot turned away.

'Strange,' he said to himself again.

The next day they did not speak much and the girl looked anxious, with dark circles under her eyes. In the afternoon the train stopped and some men came and stood by the railway line. Poirot looked out of his compartment and spoke to the conductor who was hurrying past. When he turned away, he almost walked into Mary Debenham.

'What's the matter?' she asked in a worried voice. 'Why are we stopping?'

'Some trouble under the restaurant carriage, Mademoiselle. They are repairing the damage. There is no danger.'

She waved her hand as if danger was not important.

'The *time*! We have to catch the Simplon Orient Express[2] at nine. If we are delayed arriving into Istanbul, we will miss it.'

This was strange. Her lips were shaking.

'Does it matter to you very much, Mademoiselle?' Poirot asked.

'Yes. I *must* catch that train.'

She turned away and went along the corridor to join Colonel Arbuthnot.

However, she had no need to worry. Ten minutes later the train started again and continued its journey with no problem.

Chapter 2

When they arrived in Istanbul, the passengers had to make a short ferry journey across the Bosphorus to transfer to the western side of the city. When Poirot finally reached the Tokatlian Hotel – where he was to stay for a few days – he received an unexpected message.

The event which you predicted in the Kassner <u>Case</u> has suddenly happened. Please return immediately.

'I shall have to continue my journey tonight,' Poirot said to the hotel receptionist. 'Can you get me a first-<u>class</u> sleeping carriage ticket to London on the Simplon Orient Express?'

'Certainly, Monsieur. At this time of year the trains are almost empty. I'll reserve accommodation for you in the Istanbul–Calais carriage departing at 9 pm.'

Poirot glanced at the clock. It was 7.50 pm.

'Do I have time for dinner?'

'Certainly, Monsieur.'

The little Belgian crossed the hall to the restaurant. As he was ordering his food, someone placed a hand on his shoulder.

'*Mon vieux* – my old friend, what an unexpected pleasure.'

The speaker was a short, elderly man, smiling in a delighted way. Poirot jumped up happily.

'Monsieur Bouc.'

'Monsieur Poirot.'

Monsieur Bouc was also a Belgian, a director of the Compagnie Internationale des Wagons Lits – the International Company for Sleeping Carriages. His friendship with Poirot, the former star of the Belgian Police, had begun many years earlier.

'You're far from home, *mon cher*,' said Monsieur Bouc.

'Yes, a little job in Syria.'

'Ah! And when do you return home?'

'Tonight.'

'Excellent! I'm going as far as Lausanne. I suppose you are travelling on the Simplon Orient?'

'Yes, I have just asked them to reserve me a place in a sleeping carriage.'

'Excellent. Then let's meet in the hotel reception later,' said Monsieur Bouc, before departing.

Alone again, Hercule Poirot glanced round him. There were just a few people in the restaurant and only two who interested Poirot. A young man of about thirty, obviously an American, looked pleasant. The man with him was between sixty and seventy. From a little distance his smiling mouth seemed kind, but the eyes were cruel. Not only that – the man glanced at Poirot with a very nasty look. He stood up.

'Pay the bill, Hector,' His voice was soft, but dangerous.

When Poirot joined his friend in the hotel reception, the two Americans were leaving. The younger opened the glass door.

'Ready now, Mr Ratchett.'

The older man made an angry noise.

'Hmmm,' said Poirot. 'What do you think of those two?'

'The young man seemed pleasant.' said Bouc. 'But with the other I had the opposite feeling.'

'When he passed me in the restaurant,' Poirot said, 'it was as if a wild animal had passed by.'

At that moment the receptionist arrived, looking worried.

'It's extraordinary, Monsieur Poirot. There isn't one first-class sleeping carriage free on the train.'

'*What*?' cried Bouc. 'At this time of year?' he turned to Poirot. 'Don't worry, my friend. We'll arrange something.'

At the station Monsieur Bouc was greeted with respect by the conductor.

'Good evening, Monsieur. Your compartment is number one.'

'Thank you. You're full tonight, I hear?'

'It's most surprising, Monsieur. The whole world has decided to travel tonight!'

Bouc made an annoyed sound.

'At Belgrade tomorrow there will be space in the carriage from Athens. But the problem is for tonight. Is there no second-class compartment free?'

'There is, Monsieur. But only for a lady. There is already a German woman in the compartment, you see – a lady's <u>maid</u>.'

'Don't worry, my friend,' said Poirot. 'I will travel in an ordinary carriage.'

'No, no, no,' said Bouc. He turned once more to the conductor. 'Has everyone arrived?'

'One passenger has not,' said the man. 'A Mr Harris. Compartment number seven in second-class. And we depart in four minutes...'

'Put my friend's luggage in number seven,' said Bouc. 'If Monsieur Harris arrives, tell him he's too late.'

Feeling happy, Poirot entered the train and walked along the corridor. His progress was slow, as most people were standing outside their compartments. At last he arrived at number seven. Inside was the tall young American from the Tokatlian Hotel.

As Poirot entered, the man looked annoyed.

'Excuse me, I think you have made a mistake.'

'Are you Mr Harris?' Poirot asked.

'No, my name is MacQueen. I—'

'Here you are, Monsieur,' interrupted the conductor, lifting Poirot's suitcases up onto the shelf. MacQueen said nothing more.

The train started, and the long platform moved slowly past. The Orient Express had begun its journey across Europe.

CHAPTER 3

Hercule Poirot was late entering the restaurant carriage for lunch the next day. He had got up early, had breakfast alone, and spent the morning studying the case that was taking him back to London.

Monsieur Bouc was already sitting at a table; the food was good and it was only after they had finished eating that he started to talk about other things.

'Ah!' he sighed. 'I would love to be a writer like Balzac³! I would describe all this,' he waved his hand. 'All around us are people of all levels of society, all nationalities, all ages. For three days these strangers are together. They sleep and eat under one roof. Then they go in different directions, perhaps never to see each other again.'

Poirot looked <u>thoughtfully</u> round the restaurant carriage. There were thirteen other people sitting there. At the table nearest to them, a big, dark-faced Italian was happily finishing his food. Opposite him there was a neat Englishman who looked as if he could be a <u>valet</u>. Next to him was a big American in a brightly-coloured suit.

Poirot continued looking round.

Further away, at a smaller table, sitting alone, with a very straight back, was one of the ugliest old ladies he had ever seen. However, although she was ugly, her appearance was interesting rather than unpleasant. Round her neck was a collar of very expensive jewellery. Her hands were covered with rings.

'That's Princess Dragomiroff,' said Bouc. 'Russian – and very rich.'

At another table Mary Debenham was sitting with two other women. One was tall and middle-aged with pale yellow hair tied back from her face. She wore glasses and had a long, friendly face rather like a sheep. She was listening to a large elderly woman who was talking without pausing or stopping.

'…And so my daughter said, "You just cannot use American methods in this country." But yet, our college has a fine staff of teachers. Nothing is as important as education. My daughter says—'

The train entered a tunnel – the voice was lost.

At the next table sat Colonel Arbuthnot – alone. He was looking hard at the back of Mary Debenham's head. But they were not together. Why?

Poirot glanced at the other side of the carriage, towards a middle-aged woman dressed in black with a broad face. German or Scandinavian, he thought. Probably a lady's maid. Behind her there was a couple talking together in a lively way. A big, very handsome man of about thirty with a fair moustache. The woman was young – twenty, perhaps. She wore a little black coat, a black skirt, and a white silk blouse. She had a beautiful face – white skin, large brown eyes and black hair.

'She is very beautiful,' said Poirot. 'Husband and wife?'

Bouc nodded.

'From the Hungarian embassy.'

There were only two more – MacQueen and Ratchett. Again Poirot noted those small, cruel eyes.

As coffee was brought to Poirot, Bouc stood up. He had started eating before Poirot and had finished some time ago.

'I shall return to my compartment,' he said. 'Come and have a chat later.'

'With pleasure.'

As Poirot drank his coffee, Ratchett suddenly came and sat down opposite him.

'My name is Ratchett,' he said. 'Do I have the pleasure of speaking to Hercule Poirot?'

Poirot bowed his head.

'Yes, Monsieur.'

'Mr Poirot, I want you to do a job for me.'

Hercule Poirot looked very surprised.

'Monsieur, I accept very few cases now.'

'But, Mr Poirot, I can offer you a lot of money.'

Hercule Poirot did not say anything for a moment, then he spoke:

'What do you want, Monsieur Ratchett?'

'Mr Poirot, I'm a very rich man and men in my position have enemies. Someone has <u>threatened</u> to kill me.' From his pocket he brought out a small gun for a moment. 'I am taking great care of myself. But I want to make completely sure I am safe. I think you are the man for my money, Mr Poirot. And remember – *a lot* of money.'

'I am sorry, Monsieur,' Poirot said. 'I cannot help you.'

Ratchett looked at him angrily. 'Name your price, then.'

Poirot <u>shook his head</u>.

'You do not understand, Monsieur. I have made enough money. Now I only take cases which interest me.'

'What's wrong with my offer?' Ratchett demanded.

Poirot stood up.

'I am sorry to be rude – but I do not like your face, Monsieur Ratchett.'

And he left the restaurant carriage.

CHAPTER 4

The Simplon Orient Express arrived at Belgrade at a quarter to nine that evening. Poirot stepped down onto the platform but did not stay there long. The cold was terrible and heavy snow was falling. When he returned to his compartment, the conductor was waiting for him.

'Your suitcases have been moved, Monsieur, to number one – the compartment of Monsieur Bouc.'

'But where is Monsieur Bouc?'

'He has moved into the carriage from Athens which has just been attached to the train.'

Poirot went to find his friend.

'Thank you,' he said, 'but I cannot take your compartment.'

'It's nothing,' said Bouc. 'You're going to England, so it's better that you stay in the carriage that's going all the way to Calais. I'm very happy here. It's peaceful. This carriage is empty except for myself and one Greek doctor.

'Ah! My friend, what a terrible night! They're saying there hasn't been so much snow for years. Let's hope it won't delay us.'

At 9.15 pm, the train left the station. Poirot said goodnight to his friend and went back to his own carriage.

By this time, the second day of the journey, people were getting to know each other better. Colonel Arbuthnot was at the door of his compartment talking to MacQueen.

MacQueen was surprised when he saw Poirot.

'Hey,' he called, 'I thought you'd left. Your baggage has gone.'

'Yes, it has been moved – that is all.' Poirot moved on along the corridor.

Two doors from his compartment, the loud American lady was talking to the sheep-like lady, giving her a magazine.

'Do take it, my dear. I've got a lot of things to read.' She nodded in a friendly way to Poirot.

'You are most kind, Mrs Hubbard,' said the sheep-like lady.

'Not at all. I hope your head will be better in the morning.'

'It is only a cold. I'll make myself a cup of tea.'

'Do you have some pills for your headache? Are you sure? I have more than I need. Well, goodnight, my dear.'

Mrs Hubbard turned to Poirot as the woman left.

'A nice person, she is – a Swede. She was *very* interested in what I told her about my daughter.'

Poirot, by now, knew all about Mrs Hubbard's daughter. Everyone on the train did! They knew that she and her husband were teaching at a big American college in Turkey and that this was Mrs Hubbard's first journey to the east, and what she thought of the local people and their relaxed ways.

The next door opened and Ratchett's valet stepped out. Poirot noticed Ratchett sitting in bed. He saw Poirot and his face became dark and angry. Then the door was shut.

Mrs Hubbard spoke quietly to Poirot.

'You know, there is something *wrong* about that man. My daughter says my feelings about people are always right. And I've got a feeling about that man. I don't like it. I put my suitcase against the door connecting our compartments last night because I thought I heard him trying to open the door. I'm scared of him! I don't know how that nice young man can be his secretary.'

Just at that moment, MacQueen came along the corridor with Colonel Arbuthnot.

MacQueen was saying. 'Now, what I want to understand about India is this—'

They disappeared into MacQueen's compartment.

A little later, Mrs Hubbard said goodnight and Poirot went to his compartment just on the other side of Ratchett's. He read for half an hour and then turned out the light.

Several hours later, Poirot woke with a shock. He knew what had woken him – a loud cry. At the same moment he heard a bell ring.

Poirot switched on the light. The train had stopped – he supposed they were at a station. He got out of bed and opened the door just as the conductor came hurrying along and knocked on Ratchett's door. A bell rang and a light showed over another door.

At the same moment a voice from Ratchett's compartment called:

'*Ce n'est rien. Je me suis trompé.*' It's nothing – I made a mistake.

'*Bien, Monsieur.* OK.' The conductor went quickly to the door where the light was showing.

Poirot returned to bed, glancing at his watch. It was 12.37 am.

CHAPTER 5

Poirot found it difficult to go to sleep again. Firstly, the train had stopped moving. If there *was* a station outside it was very quiet, which was strange. And secondly, the noises on the train seemed louder than usual. He could hear Ratchett moving about next door.

He heard someone walking along the corridor.

Poirot's throat felt dry. He looked at his watch again. Just after 1.15 am. He decided to ask the conductor for a bottle of water. His finger moved towards his call button, but he paused as he heard another bell ring. The man could not answer every bell at once.

The bell rang again and again. Somebody else was keeping their finger on the button.

Suddenly, Poirot heard a man hurrying along the corridor. He knocked at a door not far from Poirot's.

Then there were voices – the conductor's, speaking with respect, and a woman's – speaking many, many words.

Mrs Hubbard.

Poirot smiled to himself.

It continued for some time. Ninety per cent of the conversation was about Mrs Hubbard's troubles and ten per cent consisted of the conductor's calm voice. Finally Poirot heard clearly:

'Good night, Madame,' and a closing door. He pressed his call button. The conductor arrived quickly, looking hot and worried.

'May I have some water, please?'

'Of course, Monsieur.'

'Is anything the matter?' asked Poirot in a kind voice.

'The American lady—' replied the conductor, 'I have had a very difficult time with her! She insists there is a man in her compartment! Imagine, Monsieur. In a space of this size.' He waved a hand round.

'Where would he hide? I tell her it's impossible, but she insists. She says she woke up and there was a man there. And how, I ask, did he get out and leave the door locked behind him? But she won't listen. As if there isn't enough to worry us already. This snow—'

'Snow?'

'Oh, yes. Haven't you noticed, Monsieur? The train has stopped. There's heavy snow all around. We can't move. Nobody knows how long we'll be here.'

◆ ◆ ◆

Poirot was almost asleep when he heard the sound of a heavy object falling against his door.

He jumped from his bed and looked out of his door. To his right, further along the corridor, a woman in a red dressing-gown was walking away from him. At the other end of the corridor, sitting on his seat, the conductor was writing his daily report. Everything was quiet.

'I must be imagining things,' said Poirot and went back to bed. This time he slept till morning.

When he woke the train was still not moving. He opened the curtains of his compartment. Heavy snow surrounded the train.

Poirot got dressed and went to the restaurant carriage where he found everybody complaining. Now the passengers all shared a common problem. Mrs Hubbard's complaints were the loudest. 'We may be here for days,' she cried. 'And my boat sails the day after tomorrow. How am I going to catch it now?'

The Italian said he had urgent business in Milan.

'My sister – her children wait me,' said the Swedish lady with tears falling. 'I no contact them. They will think bad things happen to me.'

'How long will we be here?' demanded Mary Debenham. 'Doesn't anybody know?'

Her voice sounded angry, but Poirot noted that she was not as anxious as she had been during the delay to the Taurus Express.

'Excuse me, Monsieur.' A conductor stood beside him. 'Monsieur Bouc asks if you can please come to him.'

Poirot followed the man – who was not his own conductor, but a big, fair-haired man – to a compartment in the next carriage. It was crowded. Bouc was sitting in one corner. Facing him, in the other corner next to the window, was a small, dark-haired man. The train manager in a smart blue uniform, and the conductor from his own carriage were both standing up. The conductor looked as white as a ghost.

'Ah, my good friend,' cried Bouc. 'Come in. We need you.'

The dark-haired man moved along the seat. Poirot sat down facing his friend.

'What has happened?'

'That's a good question. First this snow – this stop. And now – *and now a passenger lies dead in his bed – stabbed*.' Bouc spoke with a great effort to be calm. 'An American called Ratchett.'

'Well, this is serious!' said Poirot.

'Certainly! A murder is always terrible. But we're stuck in the snow and may be here for days! When we pass through most countries we have the police of that country on the train. But not here in Yugoslavia.'

'It is a very difficult situation,' said Poirot.

'Oh, I'm sorry,' continued Bouc. 'I haven't introduced you – Dr Constantine, Monsieur Poirot.'

The little dark-haired man bowed and Poirot did the same.

'It's difficult to say exactly,' the doctor began, 'but I think that death happened between midnight and two in the morning.'

'When was the crime discovered?' asked Poirot.

'Michel, tell Monsieur Poirot what happened,' said Bouc.

The conductor's face was still pale.

'Monsieur Ratchett's valet knocked several times at his door this morning. There was no answer.' Pierre Michel's voice was shaking. 'Then, half an hour ago, the waiter from the restaurant carriage came to ask if Monsieur Ratchett would be having lunch. Still no answer.

'So I opened the door for him with my key. But there is a chain inside, too, and that was fastened. But it was very quiet and cold in there. The window was open and snow was coming in. So I got the train manager. We broke the chain and went in. He was – Oh, it was horrible!'

'Stabbed in twelve places,' announced the Greek doctor.

'That is very <u>violent</u>,' said Poirot. 'It shows that someone was very angry.'

'It's a woman,' cried the train manager. 'I'm sure about that. Only a woman would stab like that.'

There was doubt on Dr Constantine's face.

'She must have been a very strong woman. One or two of the <u>blows</u> were so powerful that they cut through bone. And yet some blows were so light they have done hardly any damage.'

'Yesterday,' said Poirot. 'Monsieur Ratchett told me his life could be in danger.'

'Then it isn't a woman,' said Bouc. 'It's a violent criminal. There's a large American on the train – a man with terrible clothes. Do you know who I mean?'

The conductor nodded.

'Yes, Monsieur, the man in number 16. But it can't have been him. I would have seen him enter or leave his compartment. It's next to my seat.'

'Well, we'll discuss it later.' Bouc looked at Poirot. 'Come, my friend, I know your abilities. Solve this case for me! It's perfect for you. Haven't you often said that to solve a case a man only has to lie back in his chair and think?' Bouc's voice became full of respect. 'Do that. Interview the passengers, go and see the body, <u>examine</u> the <u>clues</u>, use those <u>little grey cells</u> that I have heard you talk about so many times before and then – well, I'm sure you can find the answer! You will *know*!'

'Thank you, my friend,' said Poirot proudly. 'And the truth is, I find this problem interesting.'

'You accept, then?' said Bouc <u>eagerly</u>.

'I accept,' Poirot agreed.

'Good – we are all ready to help you.'

'To begin with, I would like a diagram of the Istanbul–Calais carriage, with some information about the people in each compartment. I would also like to see their passports.'

'Michel will get you those.'

'What other passengers are there on the train?' asked Poirot.

'In this carriage, Dr Constantine and I are the only travellers. The carriages on the other side are not important, since they were locked after dinner had been served. In front of the Istanbul–Calais carriage there's only the restaurant carriage.'

'When was Monsieur Ratchett last seen alive?' asked Poirot.

'He spoke to Michel at about 12.40 am,' said Bouc.

'Yes, I heard that conversation,' said Poirot.

The doctor continued.

'When we found Ratchett, the window of his compartment was open. So you would guess that the murderer escaped that way. But there were no <u>marks</u> in the snow – nobody had walked that way.'

'It was half an hour after midnight when the train hit the snow,' said Bouc. 'No one could have left the train after that, and Ratchett was alive until at least 12.40 am. So…' Bouc said in a serious voice, '*the murderer is with us – on the train now.*'

Chapter 6

'First,' said Poirot, 'I would like to have a chat with young Monsieur MacQueen.'

'Certainly,' said Bouc. He nodded to the train manager.

While they waited, the conductor returned with the passports. Bouc took them.

'Thank you, Michel. We'll interview you properly later.'

'Yes, Monsieur.' Michel left the compartment.

'After we've seen MacQueen,' said Poirot, 'perhaps *Monsieur le Docteur* will come with me to the dead man's compartment?'

'Certainly,' said Dr Constantine.

At this moment the train manager returned with Hector MacQueen.

Bouc stood up.

'There isn't much space in here,' he said pleasantly. 'Take my seat, Monsieur MacQueen.'

He turned to the train manager.

'Ask everyone to leave the restaurant carriage. Monsieur Poirot can do his interviews there.'

'That would be the most convenient place, yes,' agreed Poirot.

'What's going on?' MacQueen asked.

'Prepare yourself for a shock,' Poirot answered. '*Your employer, Monsieur Ratchett, is dead.*'

MacQueen looked surprised but he didn't seem to be upset.

'So they got him,' he said.

'You are right,' said Poirot, 'Monsieur Ratchett was murdered.' Poirot explained briefly who he was and how he was helping to find the murderer.

Then he said, 'Tell me what you know.'

'Well, I met Mr Ratchett a year ago when I was in Persia[4]. I'd come over from New York to find out more about a job with an oil company – the meeting went badly. Mr Ratchett was in the same hotel as me. He'd just had an argument with his secretary and I was glad when he offered me the job in his place.'

'And since then?'

'We've travelled about. Mr Ratchett wanted to see the world. He had difficulty because he didn't speak any languages. Honestly, I was more helpful with that than as a secretary.' The young man paused. 'He never spoke about himself, but the truth is, Mr Poirot, I don't believe Ratchett was his real name. I think he left America to escape something. And I think he was successful – until a few weeks ago.'

'And then?'

'He began to get letters that threatened to kill him. He destroyed one because he was so angry. But I've still got a couple of others. Shall I get them for you?'

'Yes, if you wouldn't mind.'

MacQueen returned with two sheets of dirty paper. Poirot examined the first:

So you thought you'd escape and we wouldn't find out, did you? No way. We're planning to GET you, Ratchett, and we WILL get you!

Poirot picked up the second letter.

We're going to kill you, Ratchett. We're going to GET you, you'll see.

Poirot put down the letters.

'Do you know when Monsieur Ratchett received the last letter?' he asked.

'On the day we left Istanbul.'

'Thank you, Monsieur MacQueen. One more question – when did you last see Monsieur Ratchett alive?'

'Yesterday evening at about 10 pm – I was in his compartment writing a letter for him.'

♦ ◆ ♦

Poirot and the doctor went to the compartment of the murdered man. The first thing they noticed was the freezing cold. The window was wide open.

'Nobody left the carriage through the window,' Poirot announced. 'Maybe the murderer wanted us to think that they did, but there are no marks in the snow. And so,' he added in a cheerful voice, 'we will shut the window!'

He turned to the bed.

Ratchett lay on his back. His <u>pyjama</u> jacket, covered with dark blood marks, had been opened.

'I had to see the <u>wounds</u>,' explained the doctor.

Poirot nodded.

'It is not pretty. How many wounds are there?'

'Twelve. One or two are very small. However, at least three were so deep that they could each have been the reason for death.'

Something in the doctor's voice made Poirot look at him.

'You think there's something strange about the wounds?'

'Yes. You see, these two – here and here. They're deep – each must have cut through his body – and yet the edges aren't open. There's been no blood.'

'What does that mean?'

'That the man was already dead when they were made. But that can't be right...'

'Hmmm,' said Poirot thoughtfully. 'Anything else?'

'Well, one thing. You see this wound here – under the right arm, near the shoulder? Could you strike a blow like that?'

Poirot raised his hand.

'I see,' said Poirot. 'With the *right* hand it is very difficult. But with the *left* hand—'

'That's right, Monsieur Poirot. That blow was struck with the *left* hand. But some of these other blows are obviously right-handed.'

'So,' said Poirot, 'we have here a First and Second Murderer. The First Murderer stabbed his <u>victim</u> and left the compartment, turning off the light. The Second Murderer came in the dark, did not see that the work had been done, and stabbed a dead body.'

'Wonderful,' said the little doctor eagerly.

Poirot's eyes shone.

'You think so? It sounded silly to me. Is there anything else that isn't normal, that might suggest there are two people involved?'

'Yes. Some of these blows, as I have said, were struck by someone who was weak. But other blows were made by a very strong person. Do you understand my point?'

'Indeed I do,' said Poirot. 'Everything is becoming beautifully clear! The murderer was a very strong man, he was weak, it was a woman, it was a right-handed person, it was a left-handed person – ah, what fun!

'And the victim, meanwhile – what does he do? Does he shout for help? Does he defend himself? No!'

He put his hand under the pillow and found the gun Ratchett had shown him.

'You see? He could have defended himself, but he did not.'

They looked around. On a small table were a glass, a bottle of water, and a dish containing a cigarette end, some paper that had been burned and two used <u>matches</u>.

The doctor picked up the glass and smelled it. 'Here is the explanation of the victim's silent death,' he said quietly.

'Was he <u>drugged</u>?'

'Yes.'

Poirot nodded. He picked up the matches. 'These are different. One is flatter than the other. You see?'

'They're the kind you get on a train,' said the doctor.

Poirot felt in the pockets of Ratchett's coat that was hanging on the wall. After a while he pulled out a box of matches. He compared them carefully with the matches in the dish.

'The rounder one is a match struck by Mr Ratchett,' he said. He looked round the compartment. With a little cry he picked up something from the floor. A small handkerchief with an embroidered initial – H.

'A woman's handkerchief,' said the doctor. 'The train manager was right. There *is* a woman involved in this.'

'And, most helpfully for us, she leaves her handkerchief!' said Poirot. 'And to make things even easier, it has an initial. How lucky we are!'

The way he spoke surprised the doctor. But Poirot had already picked up something else from the floor. This time he held out a pipe cleaner.

'Again, this was left in a most helpful way. A male clue this time. By the way, what have you done with the knife?'

'There was no knife. Ah!' the doctor had been searching the pyjama pockets of the dead man. 'I missed this.'

From the pocket he brought out a gold watch. The case was badly damaged, and the hands pointed to 1.15.

'You see?' cried Constantine eagerly. 'This shows I was right about the time of death. 1.15 am was when the crime happened.'

'It is possible, yes.'

The doctor looked at him in a curious way.

'Pardon me, Monsieur Poirot, but I don't quite understand you.'

'I do not understand myself,' said Poirot. 'I understand nothing at all, and that makes me worried.'

He sighed and looked down at the little table and the burned bits of paper.

'You see, my dear doctor, this compartment is *full* of clues. Are they real or false? I do not know yet. But here is *one* clue which I believe is *not* false. This flat match, *Monsieur le Docteur*, I believe it was used by the murderer to burn a very important paper.'

The doctor watched with interest as Poirot held up one small piece of burned paper. He could just see the pale shape of letters – three words and part of another.

'*—member little Daisy Armstrong.*'

'Ahah!' Poirot cried out in excitement. '*I know the dead man's real name. And I know why he had to leave America.*'

CHAPTER 7

They found Monsieur Bouc in the restaurant carriage.

'The real name of the victim,' said Poirot, 'was Cassetti – he is the man who murdered Daisy Armstrong.'

'That was a shocking event, I remember,' said Bouc. 'I've forgotten the details, though.'

'Colonel Armstrong was English. He married the daughter of Linda Arden, the most famous American actress at the time. They lived in America and had one child. When Daisy was three she was <u>kidnapped</u>. The Colonel paid a huge amount of money to get her back, but sadly the child's body was discovered soon afterwards – she had been dead at least a fortnight. And there was worse to follow. Mrs Armstrong was pregnant. Following the shock of Daisy's death, her child was born dead, and then she herself died. Her husband's heart was broken and he shot himself.'

'Terrible, terrible,' said Bouc. 'And I think I remember that there was also another death?'

'Yes – a French maid who the police were sure had helped the criminals. They refused to believe her when she insisted that she was <u>innocent</u>. Finally, the poor girl threw herself from a window and was killed. It was proved afterwards that she was indeed innocent.'

'That's very shocking,' said Bouc.

'About six months later, this man Cassetti was arrested as the head of the criminals who had kidnapped Daisy. But because he was very rich and had various powerful people helping him, Cassetti was never punished. He managed to disappear, and it's now clear that he changed his name and left America.'

'*Ah! Quel animal*! He really is an animal.' Bouc spoke with strong feeling. 'I'm not sorry that he's dead!'

'One member of the family is still alive – a young sister of Mrs Armstrong's,' Poirot said. 'So now we have to ask ourselves, is this a crime of private <u>revenge</u>?'

◆ ◆ ◆

Everything was ready.

Poirot and Bouc sat on one side of a table. The doctor sat at the table across from them. In front of Poirot was a diagram of the Istanbul–Calais carriage with the names of the passengers in red ink. Their passports were also on the table.

'First, the conductor,' said Poirot. 'Do you trust him?'

'Certainly. Pierre Michel has been employed by the company for fifteen years. He is <u>respectable</u> and honest.'

Poirot nodded.

'Let us interview him.'

Pierre Michel was very nervous.

'I hope Monsieur will not think that I haven't done my job properly,' he said in an anxious voice.

'No, no, of course not,' said Poirot. He then began his questions.

'What time did Monsieur Ratchett go to bed last night?'

'Immediately after dinner, Monsieur.'

'Did anybody go into his compartment afterwards?'

'His valet, Monsieur, and his secretary.'

'And was that the last time you saw him?'

'He rang his bell at about 12.40 am. I knocked, but he said he had made a mistake – *Ce n'est rien. Je me suis trompé.*'

'Yes, that was what I heard, too,' said Poirot. 'Now, Michel, where were you at 1.15 am?'

'At my seat at the end of the corridor. However, some time after one o'clock I went into the Athens carriage to speak to my colleague.'

'And when did you return?'

'One of my bells rang, Monsieur. It was the American lady.'

'I remember,' said Poirot. 'And after that?'

'I answered your bell, and another. Then I prepared the bed for Monsieur Ratchett's secretary. The English Colonel had been with him but he had just returned to his own compartment when I was called in.'

'What time was this?'

'I don't remember the exact time, Monsieur. Not later than 2 am, certainly.'

'And after that?'

'I sat in my seat till morning, Monsieur.'

'Did you see any of the passengers in the corridor?'

The man thought for a moment.

'One of the ladies went to the toilet at the end, I think.'

'Which lady?'

'I don't know, Monsieur. She had her back to me. She was wearing a red dressing-gown.'

Poirot nodded.

'And after that?'

'Nothing, Monsieur, until the morning.'

'Let us move on to another point,' Poirot said. 'If the killer did join the train last night, he could not have left it after the crime?'

'No.' Michel shook his head.

'And he cannot be hiding on the train?'

'No, it has been searched,' said Bouc. 'Forget that idea, my friend.'

'Besides,' said Michel, 'no one could get onto the sleeping carriage without me seeing them.'

Poirot did not speak for a moment.

'One other point. You said another bell rang. I heard it myself. Whose was it?'

'It belonged to *Madame la Princesse Dragomiroff*. She wanted me to call her maid.'

CHAPTER 8

For a minute or two after Pierre Michel left, Poirot continued to think hard.

'We need to have another chat with Monsieur MacQueen,' he said at last.

The young American came quickly. 'Well,' he said, 'how are things going?'

'I have learned that Ratchett, as you thought, was a false name. He was actually Cassetti, the man who kidnapped Daisy Armstrong.'

A look of great surprise appeared on MacQueen's face; then it became dark.

'The disgusting rat! I'd rather have cut off my right hand than work for him!'

'You have strong feelings, Monsieur MacQueen.'

'Monsieur Poirot, my father was the District Attorney[5] who was in charge of the case. Mrs Armstrong was a lovely woman. Cassetti deserved to die!'

'Would you have been willing to kill him yourself?'

'Yes, I—' He paused, and his cheeks became red. 'I'm making myself look <u>guilty</u>! Can I ask, how did you find out who Cassetti was?'

'From a small piece of a letter in his compartment.'

'But – I mean – that was very careless of him.'

'That depends,' said Poirot, and changed the subject.

'Now, Monsieur, we know the Colonel was in your compartment yesterday evening. Did you see anyone pass along the corridor *after* the train left Vincovci until the time Colonel Arbuthnot went to his own compartment?'

MacQueen thought.

'I think the conductor passed. And a woman.'

'Which woman?'

'I didn't really notice. I was arguing with Arbuthnot. I just remember seeing some red silk very quickly.'

Poirot nodded.

'One more question. Do you smoke a pipe?'

'No, sir.'

'Thank you, Monsieur MacQueen.' Turning to Bouc, Poirot said: 'I would now like to see Monsieur Ratchett's valet.'

♦ ◆ ♦

Edward Masterman, the English valet, arrived quickly. Poirot invited him to sit down.

'I suppose you have heard your employer has been murdered?'

'Yes, sir. A very shocking thing.'

'Tell me, please, when you last saw him.'

'Well… I went in as usual last night, sir.'

'Was he behaving in an unusual way at all?'

The valet thought for a moment.

'Well, sir, he was upset about a letter he'd been reading. He asked if I had put it in his compartment. I told him I hadn't.'

'Did your employer take any medicine to help him sleep?'

'Always, when travelling by train, sir. I gave it to him.'

'Did you know that he had enemies?'

'Yes, sir.' The man spoke without feeling. 'I heard him discussing some letters with Mr MacQueen.'

'Have you ever been to America?'

'No, sir.'

'Do you remember the Armstrong <u>kidnapping</u> case?'

Colour came into the man's cheeks.

'Oh yes, indeed, sir. A baby girl. Shocking.'

'Did you know that Monsieur Ratchett was the leader of those criminals?'

'No, sir – I had no idea.' The valet's voice was full of feeling for the first time. 'That's very difficult to believe, sir.'

'However, it is true. Now, let's talk about what you did last night. What did you do after leaving your employer?'

'I told Mr MacQueen that Mr Ratchett wanted him, sir. Then I went to my compartment and read.'

'Till when?'

'About 10.30 pm, sir. Then the other person in my compartment – a big Italian man – wanted to go to bed.'

'And then you slept?'

'I went to bed, sir, but I couldn't sleep. I had toothache. It was very painful, sir. So I continued to read – to stop me thinking about it. I went to sleep at about 4 am.'

'And the other man?'

'The Italian? Oh, he slept all night long.'

'He did not leave the compartment?'

'No, sir.'

'And how long have you been with Monsieur Ratchett?'

'Nine months, sir.'

'Thank you, Masterman. By the way, do you smoke a pipe?'

'No, sir.'

'Thank you. That's all.'

The valet paused.

'Please excuse me, sir, but the elderly American lady seems very excited. She's saying she knows all about the murderer, sir.'

'Well, then,' said Poirot, smiling, 'we should interview her next.'

♦ ◆ ♦

Mrs Hubbard arrived looking very excited and sat heavily on the seat opposite Poirot.

'I've got to tell you this. Last night the murderer was *in my compartment*! I woke up – all in the dark – and I knew there was a man in my compartment. I was so scared. I thought, "I'm going to be killed." And then, somehow, I managed to control myself and press the button for the conductor. I pressed it and pressed it – I thought my heart was going to stop. Oh! I was so happy when I heard the conductor knock on the door. "Come in," I screamed and switched on the lights. And, would you believe it, there wasn't anyone there.'

'And what happened next, Madame?'

'Well, it was obvious that the man had escaped, but it made me angry the way the conductor tried to calm me! I'm not the kind of person to imagine things, Mr Poirot. I thought it was probably the man next door – the poor man who's been killed. And I know the door between the compartments wasn't <u>bolted</u>. Well, I told the conductor to bolt it immediately.'

'And do you think this man had gone back into the compartment next door?'

'How do I know where he went? I had my eyes shut. I was so scared! The man was *right there in the compartment with me*. And I can prove it.'

In a very satisfied way, she placed a small metal object on the table.

'You see this button? I found it this morning.'

'This is a button from the jacket of an employee of the train company!' cried Bouc.

'It may have dropped from the conductor's uniform when he prepared the bed,' Poirot said gently.

'What is wrong with you people? It makes me angry when nobody believes me,' cried Mrs Hubbard.

'Madame, you have given us very important <u>evidence</u>,' said Poirot, trying to make her feel calm. 'Now, tell me – if you were nervous about Ratchett, may I ask why you had not already bolted the door between the compartments?'

'I had,' replied Mrs Hubbard. 'Well, I asked that Swedish lady if it was bolted, and she said it was.'

'You could not see for yourself?'

'No, I was in bed and my wash-bag was hanging on the door <u>handle</u>.'

'Ah. What time was this?'

'It must have been about 10.45 pm. She'd come along for a pill for her headache.'

Poirot continued: 'Do you remember the Armstrong kidnapping, Mrs Hubbard?'

'Yes, indeed I do. That animal escaped!'

'He has not escaped. He died last night.'

'*Well!*' Mrs Hubbard got up from her chair in excitement. 'Cassetti! On this train. Did I not tell you I had a feeling about that man, Mr Poirot?'

'Yes, indeed you did, Madame. And if I may, I have a personal question. It is important. Have you got a red silk dressing-gown?'

'What a strange question! No. Mine is made of pink cotton.'

Finally, as Poirot helped Mrs Hubbard towards the door, he said:

'Oh, you have dropped your handkerchief, Madame,' and held out the handkerchief with the H on it.

Mrs Hubbard looked at it.

'That's not mine, Mr Poirot. Mine have the initials C.M.H., and they're not silly expensive bits of material from Paris. What good is a handkerchief like that to anybody's nose?'

None of them had an answer to this question, and Mrs Hubbard left, feeling very satisfied.

CHAPTER 9

'This button, my friend – does it mean that Pierre Michel is involved?' Bouc asked.

'It suggests possibilities,' said Poirot thoughtfully. 'Let us speak with the Swedish lady before we discuss it.'

He looked through the passports.

'Ah! Greta Ohlsson, aged forty-nine.' Bouc spoke to the restaurant waiter, and after a while the lady with the sheep-like face came in.

She was, she told Poirot, a school nurse, at that time working near Istanbul.

'You know what happened last night, Mademoiselle?'

'Yes, it is terrible,' she said in not very good English. 'The American lady, she tell me the murderer was in her compartment.'

'Did Mrs Hubbard ask you whether the connecting door between her compartment and Monsieur Ratchett's compartment was bolted?'

'Yes, and it was. After that I go back to my own compartment, I take the headache pill and lie down.'

'The other lady in your compartment, Mademoiselle, did she leave during the night?'

'No, I don't sleep well. If the young English lady comes down from her bed, I wake up.'

Then Poirot asked: 'Do you have a red silk dressing-gown, Mademoiselle?'

'No, no.'

'And Miss Debenham? What colour is her dressing-gown?'

'Purple.'

Poirot nodded.

'And have you ever been to America, Mademoiselle?'

'No, I am sorry. They are very good, the Americans. They give much money to set up schools and hospitals.'

◆ ◆ ◆

The pleasant Swede departed and Poirot asked Pierre Michel to return.

'Michel,' said Bouc. 'Here is a button from your uniform. It was found in the American lady's compartment.'

The conductor felt his jacket. 'I haven't lost a button, Monsieur. There must be some mistake.'

The man didn't seem at all guilty or confused.

'Last night, where were you when Mrs Hubbard's bell rang?' Bouc asked.

'I told you, Monsieur – in the next carriage, talking to my colleague.'

The conductor of the next carriage was called. He said that Pierre Michel was telling the truth. The conductor from another carriage had also been there. They had discussed the snow for about ten minutes, then Michel thought he heard a bell. As he opened the doors between the carriages, they all heard it clearly, a bell ringing again and again, so Michel had run to answer it.

Both the other conductors also said they had not lost a button. And they had not been inside Mrs Hubbard's compartment.

'Michel,' said Bouc, 'when you answered Mrs Hubbard's bell, did you see anyone in the corridor?'

'No, Monsieur.'

'Strange,' said Bouc.

'It depends on the time,' said Poirot. 'Imagine. Mrs Hubbard wakes to find someone in her compartment. For a minute or two she lies unable to move, her eyes shut. It was probably then that the man went out into the corridor and then into his own compartment.'

'It's possible,' agreed Bouc. 'During the ten minutes the conductor is in the other carriage talking to his colleague, the murderer comes from his compartment, goes into Ratchett's and kills him. He locks Ratchett's door and puts a chain on it on the inside. Then he goes out through Mrs Hubbard's compartment. He's back safely in his own compartment when the conductor arrives.'

'It is not quite as simple as that, my friend,' Poirot said quietly. 'Michel, perhaps *Madame la Princesse* will be kind enough to give us a few moments of her time. Please give her that message.'

'*Oui, Monsieur.*'

Princess Dragomiroff came into the restaurant carriage and sat opposite Poirot. She was certainly ugly, and yet she had brilliant eyes, dark and proud. Her voice was loud and strong.

'I understand a murder has taken place. I'll be glad to give all the help I can.'

'You are most kind, Madame,' said Poirot. 'What is your full name and address?'

'Natalia Dragomiroff, 17 Avenue Kleber, Paris.'

'Would you mind telling me what you did last night after dinner, Madame?'

'Certainly. I went to bed immediately after dinner. I read until eleven, but then I was unable to sleep. At about 12.45 am I rang for my maid. She read aloud to me till I felt sleepy. I can't remember the exact time she left me.'

'What is your maid's name?'

'Hildegarde Schmidt.'

'Has she been with you for a long time?'

'Fifteen years.'

'Do you trust her?'

'Completely.'

Changing the subject, Poirot asked: 'You have been to America, I suppose, Madame?'

'Yes, many times.'

'Did you know the Armstrong family?'

With some feeling, the old lady said: 'You speak of friends of mine, Monsieur. I was <u>godmother</u> to Sonia Armstrong. Her mother, Linda Arden, was one of the greatest actresses in the world. She and I were very close friends.'

'Ms Arden is dead?'

'No, but she never sees anyone any more. Her health is very bad.'

'There was a second daughter, I believe.'

'Yes – she's much younger.'

'And where is she?'

The old woman gave Poirot a look.

'I must ask you how these questions are connected with the murder on this train?'

'Madame, the murdered man was <u>responsible for</u> the kidnap and murder of Mrs Armstrong's child.'

'Oh!'

Princess Dragomiroff sat up a little straighter.

'Then this murder is not such a bad thing.'

'Madame, to return to the question you did not answer: Where is the younger daughter of Linda Arden?'

'I can't tell you, Monsieur. I believe she married an Englishman but I can't remember his name.'

She paused and then said: 'Is there anything else?'

'A personal question, Madame. What colour is your dressing-gown?'

She looked surprised, then answered:

'Blue.'

'Madame, I'm very grateful to you for answering my questions,' said Poirot.

CHAPTER 10

<u>Count</u> and <u>Countess</u> Andrenyi did not arrive together as Poirot had requested. The Count entered the restaurant carriage alone.

'Monsieur Poirot, my wife and I cannot help you. We were asleep last night and heard nothing.'

'Did you know the name of the dead man, Monsieur?'

The Count looked surprised. 'Isn't it on his passport?'

'But Ratchett, Monsieur, is not his real name. He is Cassetti, the man responsible for a terrible kidnapping in America.'

The Count did not seem very shocked.

'Well,' he said, 'that should certainly make it easier to solve the crime.'

'Have you been to America, Monsieur?'

'Yes, I was in Washington for a year.'

'Then perhaps you knew the Armstrong family?'

'It's difficult to remember – I met so many people,' the Count said <u>carelessly</u>. 'What else can I do to help you, Monsieur?'

'At what time did you go to bed?'

'About 11 – the same time as my wife. I slept until morning. My wife always takes medicine to help her sleep when travelling by train, so she slept until morning, too.'

The Count stood up.

'It will be unnecessary for my wife to come here. She can't tell you anything more.'

'Of course,' said Poirot. 'But you understand, sir, it is necessary for my report.'

'Very well,' said the Count, but he did not look happy. He left the restaurant carriage.

Poirot picked up the Count's passport. Below his name, it said – *Accompanied by wife: Elena Maria; surname before marriage*

Goldenberg; age twenty. A spot of <u>grease</u> had been dropped on it by some careless person.

'A diplomatic passport[6],' said Bouc. 'We must be careful not to upset the Count.'

'Don't worry, my friend. I will be very careful.'

As the Countess Andrenyi entered the restaurant carriage, Poirot bowed politely.

'Madame, I only wish to ask if you saw or heard anything last night that may help us to understand this crime?'

'Nothing, Monsieur. I had taken a drink to help me sleep.'

'Ah! And these passport details, your mother's name and so on – they are correct?'

'Of course, Monsieur.'

'Did you go with your husband to America, Madame?'

'No, Monsieur.' Her face became a little red. 'We've only been married for a year.'

'Ah yes. Thank you, Madame. I won't delay you any longer. By the way, does your husband smoke a pipe?'

'No.'

She waited, watching him in a curious way. She had lovely dark eyes, and cheeks of smooth white skin. She looked beautiful.

'Why did you ask that?' she said.

'Madame,' Poirot waved a hand, 'detectives have to ask all sorts of questions. For instance, perhaps you will tell me the colour of your dressing-gown?'

She laughed.

'Yellow. Is that really important?'

'Very important.' Poirot bowed once more.

She smiled and left.

'A charming lady,' said Bouc.

Poirot did not reply. He was studying a grease spot on a Hungarian diplomatic passport.

♦ ◆ ♦

'Are you coming home from India on holiday – what we call *en permission?*' Poirot asked.

Colonel Arbuthnot was not interested in what the Europeans called anything. He gave the short answer typical of a British person.

'Yes.'

'But you are not coming home by boat?'

'No, I chose to travel across land, stopping in Baghdad to see an old friend.'

'Miss Debenham has also come from Baghdad. Perhaps you met her there?'

'No. I first met Miss Debenham a few days ago on the Taurus Express train.'

'Let us talk about the crime. We believe it took place at 1.15 am.'

'Well, at 1.15 am I was talking to the American – the secretary to the dead man – in his compartment.'

'Is Monsieur MacQueen a friend?'

'No. I'd never met him before yesterday. But he was interested in India. And I was interested in the financial situation in America. Then we discussed world politics in general. I was surprised to look at my watch and find it was 1.45 am.'

'That is the time you went to your compartment?'

'Yes.'

'Where was the conductor?'

'Sitting at the end of the corridor.'

'Now, Colonel Arbuthnot, I need to know about the time after the train left Vincovci. You got out of the train then, I think?'

'Yes, but only for a minute. There was a snowstorm.'

'Will you think back, please? You come and sit down in Monsieur MacQueen's compartment. You smoke, perhaps?'

'Yes, a pipe for me; MacQueen smoked cigarettes.'

'The train starts again. It is late now. Most people have gone to bed for the night. Does anyone pass the door?'

Arbuthnot thought hard.

'I remember the conductor. And there was a woman, I think. I wasn't looking that way. I just smelled some perfume. It was quite strong.'

'And tell me, have you ever been to America, Colonel Arbuthnot?'

'Never.'

'Did you ever know a Colonel Armstrong?'

'I've known two or three Armstrongs.'

'I mean the Colonel Armstrong whose only child was kidnapped and killed.'

'Ah, yes, I read about that – a shocking case. Of course, I knew *of* him. Toby Armstrong had a very successful career.'

'Well, Colonel, the man who was killed last night was the man responsible for the murder of Colonel Armstrong's child.'

Arbuthnot's face grew very serious.

'Then the rat deserved what he got. Though I would have preferred to see him punished by the <u>law</u>.'

'You prefer the law to private revenge, Colonel?'

'Well, trial by jury[7] is a good and fair method.'

Chapter 11

Mr Hardman, the big American, was wearing a suit with a bright pattern and had a piece of chewing gum in his mouth. His face was large and friendly.

'Morning, sir. What can I do for you?'

Poirot looked at his passport.

'You are Cyrus Hardman, salesman, travelling from Istanbul to Paris?'

'Yes, that's me.'

'What can you tell us about the events of last night?'

The American thought for a minute.

'I think I should tell you everything.'

'It will certainly be best for you to tell us all you know,' said Poirot.

'*If* there was anything I *did* know. But I don't. I know nothing. But I *should* know something. It makes me angry.'

Poirot looked confused. 'Please explain, Monsieur Hardman.'

Mr Hardman sighed, removed the chewing gum, and put his hand in one of his pockets. He seemed to change and become more like a real person.

'That passport's false,' he said, passing Poirot a business card. 'This is who I really am.'

Poirot looked at the card carefully. Bouc looked over his shoulder.

CYRUS B. HARDMAN
MCNEIL'S DETECTIVE AGENCY
NEW YORK.

Poirot knew the name. It was one of the best private detective agencies in New York.

'I came over to Europe following a couple of criminals to Istanbul. Then I got this.'

Mr Hardman pushed a letter across the table.

The paper was from the Tokatlian hotel.

Dear Sir,
I have been informed that you are a detective working for McNeil's Detective Agency. Please come to my room at four o'clock this afternoon.
S.E. Ratchett.

'I went. Mr Ratchett showed me a couple of letters he'd received. He asked me to do a job and I said yes. He wanted me to travel by the same train and see that nobody got him. Well, in spite of me, somebody *did* get him. I certainly feel bad about it.'

'Did he give you an idea of how he wanted you to work?'

'Sure. Compartment 16 seemed a pretty good position. There was only the restaurant carriage in front of our carriage, and the door to the platform at the front end was locked at night. The only way a killer could come was past my compartment – and I knew what he looked like.'

'What?'

Poirot, Bouc and Constantine were all listening eagerly.

'Mr Ratchett described him to me – a small man, dark-haired, with a voice like a woman. He said he didn't believe it would be the first night. More likely the second or third.'

'So he knew something,' said Bouc.

'He certainly knew more than he told his secretary,' said Poirot thoughtfully. He glanced at Hardman. 'You knew who Ratchett really was, of course?'

'I don't know what you mean.'

'Ratchett was Cassetti, the Armstrong murderer.'

Mr Hardman made a surprised noise.

'Yes, *of course*! I didn't recognize him – I was away at that time. Well, I'm sure that a lot of people wanted Cassetti dead.'

'Continue your story, Monsieur Hardman.'

'There's very little to tell. I slept in the day and had my door open a little at night. No stranger passed. Nobody got on that train and nobody came along from the carriage at the back. I'm quite sure about that.'

♦ ◆ ♦

The Italian, Antonio Foscarelli, came into the restaurant carriage, walking like a cat. He had a bright sunny smile on his face.

'I see from your passport that you have become a citizen[8] of America, Monsieur?' said Poirot.

'Yes, it's better for my business.'

'You work for Ford cars?'

'Yes—'

A long story followed. At the end of it, the three men knew everything about Foscarelli's business and his opinion of the United States. His kind face had a satisfied smile.

'In the United States, did you ever meet Ratchett?' Poirot asked.

'Never. But I know that type of person. Oh, yes. Well-dressed – but underneath, all wrong. I'd guess he was probably a big criminal.'

'You are quite right,' said Poirot. 'Ratchett was Cassetti, the man who kidnapped little Daisy Armstrong.'

'Ahah! What did I tell you?'

'Did you know the Armstrong family?'

'No.'

'Tell me, did the other man in your compartment leave during the night?

'Oh, the English are miserable people. Last night he sits in the corner reading, always with a sad face. Then the conductor prepares our beds. Mine is the upper bed. I get up there. I smoke my cigarette and read. The little Englishman has toothache, I think. He has a small bottle of stuff that smells very strong. He lies in bed and makes noises of pain. After a while, I sleep. If he leaves I would hear. The light from the corridor – it wakes you up.'

When the Italian left, his smile was still bright.

'He has been in America for a long time so he could have known the Armstrongs,' said Bouc, 'and Italians use a knife!'

'Certainly,' said Poirot, 'particularly when they get angry during a fight. But this is a different kind of crime, my friend. I think this crime was carefully planned. It shows a calm, clever mind.'

He picked up the last two passports.

'Let us now see Miss Mary Debenham.'

◆ ◆ ◆

Mary Debenham entered the restaurant carriage, dressed in a smart black suit and seeming very calm.

'Mademoiselle, what do you have to say to us about what happened last night?' began Poirot.

'Nothing, I'm afraid. I went to bed and slept.'

'Aren't you upset, Mademoiselle, that a crime has happened on this train?'

The question was clearly unexpected. Her grey eyes became wide.

'No, I can't say I'm upset.'

'A crime – it is quite a normal thing for you, eh?'

'Well, it is unpleasant,' said Mary Debenham. 'But people die every day.'

Poirot looked at her in a curious way.

'Do you know who Ratchett really was, Mademoiselle?'

She nodded.

'Mrs Hubbard has been telling everyone.'

'You did not know the dead man?'

'No, I saw him for the first time yesterday.'

'And what do you think of the Armstrong case?'

'It was terrible,' said the girl quietly.

'You do not have strong feelings about it, Mademoiselle?'

'Monsieur Poirot, I'm afraid I can't get upset just to prove to you that I have feelings.'

Poirot looked at her thoughtfully.

'Are you returning to Baghdad after your holiday?'

'I don't know yet. I'd prefer to find a job in London.'

'I see. I thought, perhaps, you might be getting married.'

Miss Debenham did not reply. But her look clearly said: 'You are very rude.'

Poirot continued. 'The lady who is with you in your compartment, Mademoiselle Ohlsson, what colour is her dressing-gown?'

Mary Debenham looked at him in surprise.

'Brown.'

'Ah! And yours is purple, I believe.'

'Yes.'

'Do you have another dressing-gown, Mademoiselle? A red one?'

'No, that isn't mine.'

Ahah! Miss Debenham knew that there was a red dressing-gown. Poirot was like a cat catching a mouse.

'Whose is it, then?'

The girl sat back a little, surprised by the excitement in Poirot's voice.

'I don't know. I woke up this morning at about 5 am with the train standing still. I looked out into the corridor, thinking we might be at a station. I saw someone in a red dressing-gown at the other end of the corridor.'

'Did she have fair, dark, or grey hair?'

'I don't know. She was wearing a hat.'

'What about her shape?'

'Tall and slim, I'd say.'

Poirot was quiet for a minute. He said to himself:

'I cannot understand any of this.'

Then, looking up, he said:

'Thank you, Mademoiselle.'

CHAPTER 12

'Ah, well,' said Poirot, picking up the last passport, 'to the final name on our list. The maid.'

Hildegarde Schmidt seemed calm, respectable – though perhaps not very intelligent.

Poirot spoke to her in a very kind way.

'We want to know as much as possible about last night,' he said gently.

She continued looking calm but rather stupid.

'I do not know anything, Monsieur.'

'Well, for one thing, you know that Princess Dragomiroff sent for you?'

'That, yes.'

'Was it unusual for her to send for you in this way?'

'No, Monsieur. My lady does not sleep well.'

'Did you put on a dressing-gown?'

'No, Monsieur, I got dressed. I would not go to Madame in my dressing-gown.'

'But you have a very nice dressing-gown – it's red, is it not?'

She looked at him in surprise.

'It's dark blue, Monsieur.'

'Ah! Continue.'

'I read aloud to Madame. When she became sleepy, I returned to my own compartment.'

'And in the corridor you did not see a lady in a red dressing-gown?'

Her kind eyes opened wide in surprise.

'No, indeed, Monsieur. There was nobody except the conductor. He came out of one of the compartments.'

'Which compartment?' Poirot asked, not letting his excitement show.

'It was in the middle of the carriage, Monsieur. He nearly walked into me.'

'Which direction was he going in?'

'Towards me, Monsieur. He apologized and went on towards the restaurant carriage. A bell began ringing, but I don't think he answered it.'

'This poor conductor seems to have had a busy night,' Poirot said. 'First waking you and then answering bells.'

'It wasn't the same conductor who woke me, Monsieur. It was another one.'

'Ah! Would you recognize him?'

'I think so, Monsieur.'

Poirot nodded to Bouc who went to the door to call the conductor.

Poirot continued.

'Have you ever been to America, Madame Schmidt?'

'Never, Monsieur.'

He handed her the handkerchief.

'Is this yours, Madame Schmidt?'

A little colour came into her face.

'No, Monsieur. It is a lady's handkerchief. Very expensive, embroidered by hand in Paris.'

'You do not know whose it is?'

'Me? Oh, no, Monsieur.'

Of the three men who were listening, only Poirot noticed the small delay in her reply.

Bouc spoke into Poirot's ear. Poirot nodded and said to the woman:

'The three conductors are coming in. Will you tell me which one came to get you last night?'

The three men entered. They were Pierre Michel, the big blond conductor from the Athens–Paris carriage, and the large conductor from the Bucharest carriage.

Hildegarde Schmidt shook her head.

'None of these, Monsieur. The one I saw was small and dark-haired. He had a little moustache. His voice when he said *"Pardon"* was weak, like a woman's. I remember him very well, Monsieur.'

◆ ◆ ◆

The conductors and Hildegarde Schmidt had gone.

'I don't understand!' said Bouc. 'The enemy that Ratchett spoke of – how can he have disappeared? I feel very confused. Please explain to me what happened.'

'Dear friend, the progress of this case is very strange.'

'There's no progress at all.'

Poirot shook his head.

'No, that is not true. We know some things for sure. We hear about the small dark-haired man with a voice like a woman's from Hardman. Hildegarde Schmidt's description of the man in uniform matches it. And there is the button found by Madame Hubbard. Both Colonel Arbuthnot and Hector MacQueen say the conductor passed their carriage. But *Pierre Michel has said he did not leave his seat except for a few times.*

'Therefore this story of a small dark-haired man in uniform depends on these four people who saw him.'

'Yes, yes, my friend,' Bouc said. 'We all agree that this person exists. The question is – *where did he go?*'

Poirot shook his head.

'You are making a mistake. Before I ask myself, "Where did this man go?" I ask myself, "Did this man really exist?" You see, if the man were not real, it would be much easier for him to disappear!'

'But that's mad!'

'It is so mad, my friend, that sometimes I think that really it must be very simple,' said Poirot in a cheerful voice. 'Last night on the train there are two strangers. There is the conductor, and there is also a tall, slim woman in a red dressing-gown. She, too, has disappeared. Where are they, these two? And where are the uniform and the red dressing-gown?'

'Ah!' Bouc jumped up eagerly. 'We must search the passengers' luggage.'

Poirot stood up too.

'I will predict,' he said, 'that you will find the uniform in the baggage of Hildegarde Schmidt.'

'You think—'

'I will say it like this. If Hildegarde Schmidt is guilty, the uniform *might* be found in her baggage – but if she is innocent it *certainly* will be.'

'But—' began Bouc, and then stopped.

'What's that noise?' he cried.

The noise consisted of loud cries in a woman's voice. Suddenly, the door opened and Mrs Hubbard pushed her way in.

'It's just too horrible,' she cried. 'In my wash-bag. A huge knife – *covered with blood!*' And she fell forwards onto Bouc's shoulder.

CHAPTER 13

Every traveller on the train seemed to be outside Mrs Hubbard's compartment. The conductor was keeping them back.

'Monsieur Poirot,' said the conductor as Poirot, Bouc and Constantine approached. 'The American lady – all those loud screams. I thought she'd been murdered too!'

He added, waving his hand:

'*It* is in there, Monsieur. I haven't touched it.'

Poirot entered the compartment. Hanging on the handle of the door connecting with the next compartment was a large wash-bag. Below it on the floor was a knife. It was a type that anyone could buy in Istanbul.

Poirot picked it up.

'Yes,' he said. 'Here is our missing knife – eh, Docteur?'

The doctor examined it.

'You do not need to be so careful,' said Poirot. 'There will be no <u>fingerprints</u> on it except Madame Hubbard's.'

'It could certainly have made all of the wounds,' Constantine said.

Poirot looked thoughtfully at the door, at the wash-bag and at the door <u>bolt</u> which was a little above the handle.

'Ah, I understand now,' said Bouc. 'The man enters through the door connecting the compartments. He puts the knife inside the wash-bag, then goes out through the other door into the corridor.'

'Yes,' said Poirot very quietly. But he still looked confused.

Mrs Hubbard came in, looking very nervous.

'I wouldn't sleep in this compartment tonight if you paid me a million dollars,' she cried. 'Next door to a dead man! I would go mad.'

She began to cry.

'Madame,' Poirot said calmly before she could say any more, 'you will be taken immediately to another compartment in the other carriage.'

Mrs Hubbard put her handkerchief down.

'Oh, I feel better just hearing you say that.'

'And it would be better for Madame to have a different number this time,' suggested Poirot to the conductor. 'Number 12, perhaps.'

'*Bien*, Monsieur,' replied Michel, and he began to move the baggage immediately.

Mrs Hubbard was accompanied to her new home by Poirot. She looked around her happily.

'What still makes me confused, Madame,' said Poirot, 'is how the man got into your compartment. The door connecting the compartments was locked, you say. But you were lying in your bed and could not see the bolt yourself?'

'No, because of the wash-bag.'

Poirot hung the wash-bag on the handle of the door.

'I see,' he said. 'The bolt is just underneath the handle – the wash-bag hides it. You could not see it.'

'That's what I've been telling you!'

'The Swedish lady may have made a mistake, Madame. Perhaps she tried to open the door, and it was locked from Mr Ratchett's compartment on the other side. So she believed it was locked on your side.'

'Well, I suppose...'

'Now, you have had a shock, Madame. You must rest. But first, would you mind if I search your baggage?'

'Why?'

'We are about to search all the passengers' luggage. I do not want to remind you of an unpleasant experience, but your wash-bag – remember?'

'You're right! Perhaps you'd better search my luggage! I certainly don't want any more surprises of that type.'

♦ ♦ ♦

The search was over quickly. Next was Mr Hardman. He was smoking a cigarette and welcomed them. He was friendly and helpful.

'Please come in. To tell the truth, I've been wondering why you didn't do this search sooner. Things are done much faster in America.'

'It is true that America is the country of progress,' agreed Poirot. 'There is much that I respect about Americans. However, I find American women less charming than French or Belgian girls.'

Hardman turned away to look out at the snow for a minute.

'Perhaps you're right, Monsieur Poirot.' He shut his eyes quickly for a moment as though the snow hurt them. 'It's a bit bright, isn't it?'

Like most Army men, Colonel Arbuthnot was very neat in the way he packed his bags. The search took only minutes but Poirot noted a packet of the same pipe cleaners as the one he had found in the dead man's compartment.

At the next compartment, Bouc was very polite as he explained to Princess Dragomiroff that they wanted to search her luggage.

'My maid has the keys,' she answered. 'She will do what you need.'

When Hildegarde Schmidt arrived, the princess told her to open the suitcases. She herself stood in the corridor looking out at the snow. Poirot stood with her.

She looked at him with a smile.

'Well, Monsieur, don't you want to see what's in my suitcases?'
He shook his head.

'Madame, in your case there is no need.'

'And yet I knew and loved Sonia Armstrong. And Cassetti – do you know what I'd like to have done? To have told my employees: "Beat this man to death and throw him out like rubbish." That's the way things were done when I was young, Monsieur.'

Then she turned suddenly back to her compartment. The search was over – they had found nothing of interest.

The doors of the next two compartments were shut. Bouc paused.

'These two are travelling on diplomatic passports. Their baggage can't be touched.'

'Do not worry, my friend. The Count and Countess will agree to help us.' And Poirot gave a loud knock on the door.

A voice cried, '*Entrez* – Come in!'

The Count was reading a newspaper. The Countess was sitting near the window. She seemed to have been asleep.

'Please forgive us for interrupting you,' began Poirot. 'We are searching the baggage. Bouc suggests that, as you have a diplomatic passport, you might refuse to let us do this search—'

'Thank you,' the Count said. 'But I'd prefer our baggage to be searched like that of the other passengers.'

They started the search quickly.

'This label on your suitcase is wet, Madame,' Poirot said as he lifted down a blue leather case.

The Countess did not reply. She seemed bored by everything.

As they moved along the corridor, they passed Mrs Hubbard's old compartment, that of the dead man, and then Poirot's. After these was the second-class compartment where Mary Debenham and Greta Ohlsson were situated. The Swedish lady seemed worried and upset. Mary Debenham, on the other hand, showed a complete lack of interest.

Poirot spoke to the Swedish lady.

'If you permit it, Mademoiselle, we will look at your baggage first. Then would you mind seeing how the American lady is getting on? She is still very upset.'

Miss Ohlsson was pleased to help. She said she would go immediately – they could search her case while she was away. She hurried off and they were soon finished with her suitcases.

As Poirot opened one of Miss Debenham's cases, she said:

'How clever you are, Monsieur Poirot. You sent her away because you wanted me alone. So much time is wasted by not being honest about things.'

'And you like the honest method, Mademoiselle. Therefore, I will give it to you. On our journey from Syria you said to Colonel Arbuthnot, "Not now. When it is all over." What did you mean, Mademoiselle?'

She said very quietly:

'Do you think I meant murder?'

'You tell me, Mademoiselle.'

She sighed.

'Monsieur, those words were about a promise I made.'

'A promise you have now completed?'

'Why do you think that?'

'Well, our train was delayed on the day we were to reach Istanbul. You were very worried.'

For the first time, Miss Debenham looked angry.

'Well, delay can spoil plans and create a lot of problems.'

'And yet – it is strange – we have a delay again now and there is no way to contact your friends. Yet *this* time, Mademoiselle, you are not worried. You are calm.'

Mary Debenham's face became red and she bit her lip. She said in a cold voice:

'I have nothing more to say.'

'It does not matter,' said Hercule Poirot. 'I will find out.' He bowed and left the compartment.

'Was that sensible, my friend?' asked Bouc. ' From now on, she's going to be very careful.'

'If you wish to catch a rabbit you put a <u>ferret</u> into the hole. If the rabbit is there, he runs. That is all I have done.'

They now entered the compartment of Hildegarde Schmidt. She was standing ready.

'It isn't locked, Monsieur.'

Poirot opened the suitcase and lifted the lid.

'Ahah!' he said to Bouc, 'do you remember what I said? Look!'

On the top of the suitcase was a brown conductor's uniform.

The German woman was suddenly no longer calm.

'Ach!' she cried. 'That is not mine. I haven't looked in that case since we left Istanbul.' She looked at Poirot, very nervous and upset.

'There is no need to worry,' said Poirot. 'Everything is fine. We believe you. This man you saw in the conductor's uniform, he comes out of the dead man's compartment and there you are. That is bad luck for him. He hoped no one would see him. He must get rid of his uniform. It is now a danger for him.'

He glanced at Bouc and Dr Constantine.

'The snow, you see, confuses all his plans. Where can he hide these clothes? He passes an open door, an empty compartment. It must belong to the woman he has just seen walking away.

So he goes in, takes off his uniform and pushes it quickly into a suitcase.'

Poirot held up the jacket. The third button down was missing. He felt in the pockets and took out a conductor's key.

'That is how our man was able to pass through locked doors,' said Bouc.

'Now,' said Poirot, 'we just have to find the red dressing-gown.'

Hector MacQueen welcomed them next.

'It's good you're searching,' he said with a sad smile. 'I feel I'm the most suspicious person on the train. If you find a document in which the old man said he was going to leave me his money after he died, I'll be in real trouble.'

Bouc gave him a suspicious look.

'I'm joking,' said MacQueen quickly. 'He'd never have left me any money. I was just useful to him – languages and so on. He didn't speak anything except American.'

They found nothing of interest in MacQueen's luggage, so they moved on to the last compartment. The luggage of the big Italian and of the valet Masterman also showed them nothing.

'What next?' asked Bouc.

'We will go back to the restaurant carriage,' said Poirot. 'We have all the evidence. Now we use our brains.'

He felt in his pocket for his cigarette case. It was empty. 'I will join you in a moment.'

He hurried along the corridor to his own compartment – he had more cigarettes in one of his suitcases.

He opened the lock.

Then he looked hard in surprise.

Neatly folded in his case was a red silk dressing-gown.

'So,' he said. 'A challenge. Very well. I accept it.'

CHAPTER 14

When Poirot entered the restaurant carriage, Bouc was looking sad.

'If you solve this case, dear friend, I will really believe in <u>miracles</u>!'

'I agree,' said the doctor.

'Don't be depressed,' said Poirot. 'We have the evidence of the passengers and the evidence of our own eyes – there are several points of interest. Take these very important words of the young MacQueen: "We've travelled about. Mr Ratchett wanted to see the world. He had difficulty because he did not speak any languages."'

He looked from the doctor to Bouc.

'What? You still do not understand? You had a second chance just now when he reminded us that Ratchett needed him for his language abilities.'

Bouc still looked confused.

'My dear friend, *Ratchett spoke no French.* Yet, when the conductor answered his bell last night, he was told he was not wanted – *in French. "Ce n'est rien. Je me suis trompé."* It's nothing. I made a mistake.'

'It's true,' cried Constantine excitedly. 'Now I see why we cannot depend on the evidence of the damaged watch. At 12.37 am Ratchett was already dead—'

'And it was his murderer speaking!' finished Bouc.

Poirot raised a hand.

'Let us not say more than we know. It is safe to say that *some other person* was in Ratchett's compartment.'

'Oh, you are very careful, my friend,' said Bouc.

'We have no real *evidence* that Ratchett was dead at that time. We should go forwards slowly. I have made a list,' Poirot handed him a sheet of paper:

Things needing explanation.

The handkerchief with the initial H. Whose is it?

The pipe cleaner. Was it dropped by Colonel Arbuthnot? Or someone else?

Who wore the red dressing-gown?

Who was the man or woman in uniform?

Why do the hands of the watch point to 1.15?

Was that the time of the murder?

Was it earlier?

Was it later?

Can we be sure that Ratchett was stabbed by more than one person?

What other explanation of his wounds can there be?

Poirot sat back in his seat. 'From now on, it is all here,' he touched himself on the forehead. 'The facts are all in front of us. Let us close our eyes and think.'

◆ ◆ ◆

Hercule Poirot sat without moving. He looked like he was asleep.

After a quarter of an hour of complete silence, he sighed and said quietly:

'Ah, that would explain everything.'

His eyes opened. They were green like a cat's.

'Well, well, well.' Poirot sat up straight in his chair. 'My friends, I find a strange explanation. But to be sure that it is true, I need to do an experiment.

'So let us start with a fresh grease spot on a Hungarian passport.'

The two men looked at him in surprise.

Bouc picked up the passport of Count and Countess Andrenyi.

'Is this what you mean? This dirty mark?'

'Yes. You see where it is?'

'At the beginning of the Countess's name.'

'Let us go back to the handkerchief that was found where the crime took place. It is, my friends, very expensive, so I believe there are just two women on the train who could own a handkerchief like this. Can we connect them with the letter H? The two are Princess Dragomiroff—'

'Whose name is Natalia,' interrupted Bouc.

'Yes, indeed. And the other is Countess Elena Andrenyi. And her name on the passport has a little spot of grease on it. Just think about that name, Elena. Suppose instead it were *Helena*. That capital H could be turned into a capital E and then cover the small e next to it easily – and then a spot of grease dropped to hide the change.'

'Helena,' cried Bouc. 'That's an interesting idea.'

'Certainly! So I looked for evidence that my idea is true – and I found it. One of the luggage labels on the Countess's baggage is a little wet. It has been removed with water and stuck on top of the case again in a different place – to cover the first initial of the name Helena.'

'But the Countess Andrenyi,' said Bouc. 'I can't believe—'

'Ah, now, my friend, you must ask yourself a different question: How was this murder *meant* to appear to everybody? Do not forget that the snow changed the murderer's plan. Imagine there is no snow. What happens?

'The murder is discovered early in the morning at the Italian border. Almost the same evidence is given to the Italian police. I imagine only two things are different. The man passes through Mrs Hubbard's compartment before one o'clock – and the uniform is found in one of the toilets.'

'You mean…?'

'I mean the murder was *planned to look like it was done by somebody from outside – somebody who had come onto the train.* They wanted us to think that the killer had left the train at Brod, when the train arrived there at 12.58 am. Somebody would probably say that they passed a strange conductor in the corridor. That, my friends, was how the crime was intended to look.

'But the snow changes everything. It stops us, we don't reach Brod, and the murderer is now *known* to be still on the train.'

'Yes, yes,' said Bouc. 'But what about the handkerchief?'

'I will return to it, but wait. First, you must realize that the threatening letters that Ratchett received are not real – they were just intended for the police. Ratchett certainly received *one* letter – one that names the Armstrong baby. This was to make sure he understood that his life was in danger. That letter was *not* supposed to be found – but we found it. This was the second way that the murderer's plans went wrong. The first was the snow; the second was when we found that piece of the note.

'There can only be one reason why that note was destroyed. *There must be someone on this train so closely connected with the Armstrong family that the note would immediately make us <u>suspect</u> that person.*

'Now to the handkerchief: if we look at it in the simplest way possible, it means someone whose initial is H is guilty.'

'Yes, exactly,' said Dr Constantine. 'The Countess realizes she has dropped the handkerchief and so she hides her first name.'

'No, no, the grease spot and the changed label only prove that the Countess Andrenyi wants to hide who she is. It should not be difficult to guess her real name. Mrs Armstrong's mother was Linda Arden, an actress. But Arden was her professional name, so her daughters did not share it. I suggest, my friends, that the younger sister of Mrs Armstrong, who was just a child at the time of the kidnapping, was Helena Goldenberg – now Countess Helena Andrenyi. She is the younger daughter of Linda Arden. She married Count Andrenyi when he was working at the Hungarian Embassy in Washington.'

'But Princess Dragomiroff says that she married an Englishman,' pointed out Constantine.

'Yes, whose name she cannot remember! I ask you, my friends – is that likely? Princess Dragomiroff was godmother to one of Linda's daughters. Would she forget the married name of the other daughter? No, Princess Dragomiroff was lying.'

At dinner the people in the restaurant carriage were very quiet. Poirot had spoken to the head waiter and the Count and Countess were served last, then there was a delay in preparing their bill. Therefore they were the last to leave the restaurant carriage.

Poirot jumped up and followed them.

'Excuse me, Madame, you have dropped your handkerchief.'

She glanced at it. 'You're wrong, Monsieur, that isn't mine.'

'And yet, Madame, it has your initial – H.'

The Count moved forwards suddenly. Poirot did not pay him any attention. The Countess looked hard at Poirot.

'Monsieur, my initials are E.A.'

'I think not. Your name is Helena – not Elena. Helena Goldenberg, the sister of Mrs Sonia Armstrong.'

The faces of both the Count and Countess had become white. The Count said angrily:

'Monsieur, I demand to know how you think you can—'

The Countess interrupted him.

'No, Rudolph, it's better to talk.'

Her voice had changed. It was still strong, but now she spoke with an American accent.

They both sat down opposite Poirot.

'It's true – I am the younger sister of Mrs Armstrong,' said the Countess.

'Will you tell me why you changed your passport?'

Helena said quietly:

'Surely, Monsieur Poirot, you can guess. This man who was killed, he murdered my baby niece, killed my sister, broke her husband's heart. Three of the people I loved best – they were my whole world!'

Her voice was full of feeling but now she continued more quietly.

'Of all the people on the train, I had the best reason for killing him. But I promise you, Monsieur Poirot, that, although I've always wanted to, I never touched that man.'

'And I promise you that's true,' said the Count. 'Last night Helena never left her compartment. She is innocent.'

Poirot shook his head.

'And yet you changed the name in the passport?'

'I did it,' the Count said with feeling. 'We heard about the handkerchief with the letter H. Monsieur Poirot, do you think I wanted my wife to be involved in an awful police case? Suspected, interviewed, arrested perhaps, because some bad luck had put us on the same train as this man. She was innocent. Monsieur, I admit I lied to you – but I was telling the truth when I said that my wife never left her compartment last night.'

He spoke in such an honest way that it was hard not to believe him.

The girl said, 'The handkerchief is not mine, Monsieur. I was scared. It had been so awful – and to be reminded about it all again was terrible. I was horribly scared, Monsieur Poirot. Can't you understand that?'

Her voice was lovely – the voice of the daughter of Linda Arden, the actress.

Poirot looked at her seriously.

'If you want me to believe you, Madame, then help me. The reason for the murder lies in that terrible event. Take me back into the past, so that I may find that reason.'

'What can I say? They are all dead. Robert, Sonia, Daisy. She was so sweet, so happy.'

'There was another victim, Madame.'

'Poor Susanne? Yes, the police were sure she was involved in it. Perhaps she was – but I believe only in an innocent way. I think she just talked with someone about the time that Daisy was usually taken out. But she felt responsible for what happened, and she— she jumped out of a window.'

The Countess covered her face with her hands.

'What nationality was she, Madame?'

'French.'

'What was her last name?'

'It's silly, but I can't remember – we all called her Susanne. A pretty, laughing girl. She loved Daisy.'

'And she looked after her?'

'Yes.'

'Who was the nurse?'

'Her name was Stengelberg.'

'You were only a young girl at the time too – did you have someone to look after you?'

'Oh, yes, I had an older lady – a sort of governess who was also a secretary to Sonia. She was English – no, Scottish. A big, red-haired woman.'

'What was her name?'

'Miss Freebody.'

CHAPTER 15

'You see?' said Poirot, when the Count and Countess had gone. 'We are making progress.'

'Excellent work,' said Bouc eagerly. 'I would never have suspected Countess Andrenyi.'

'Do you not believe the Count, that his wife is innocent?'

'Oh, it must be a lie. He loves his wife. He wants to save her.'

'Actually, I believe it is the truth. I told you there were two possible owners of the handkerchief.'

'Yes, but—' Bouc stopped as Princess Dragomiroff entered the restaurant carriage.

She spoke to Poirot, paying no attention to the others.

'I believe, Monsieur, that you have a handkerchief of mine.'

Poirot looked with pleasure at the other two. He took the handkerchief from his pocket.

'It has my initial in the corner.'

'But, *Madame la Princesse*, that is the letter H,' said Bouc. 'Your name is Natalia.'

She gave him a cold look.

'That is correct, Monsieur. My handkerchiefs are embroidered with Russian initials. H is N in Russian.'

Bouc was very surprised.

'Messieurs, your next question will be – why was my handkerchief lying beside a murdered man? My reply is that I have no idea.'

'Please excuse me, Madame,' Poirot said very gently. 'But how can we believe you?'

Princess Dragomiroff answered as if the question was unimportant.

'I suppose you mean because I didn't tell you that Helena Andrenyi was Mrs Armstrong's sister?'

'Yes. You lied to us.'

'Certainly, and I would do the same again. Her mother was my friend. I believe in protecting my friends.'

'Your maid, Madame, recognized this handkerchief when we showed it to her.'

'Of course she recognized it. Did she not say anything? Well, she showed that she, too, can protect people.'

She bowed her head a little and left the restaurant carriage.

'Ah!' said Bouc, 'she's a terrible old lady!'

'But could she have murdered Ratchett?' Poirot asked the doctor. He shook his head.

'Those blows were very violent. No-one so weak could ever strike them.'

'But the ones that were less deep…?'

Bouc shook his head, confused.

'Lies – and again lies. It surprises me greatly, the number of lies we've been told.'

'Oh, there are more still to discover,' said Poirot in a cheerful voice.

◆ ◆ ◆

Colonel Arbuthnot was clearly annoyed at being called to the restaurant carriage for a second time. His face was unfriendly as he sat down.

'Why did you call me?'

'To begin with,' said Poirot, 'is this pipe cleaner yours?'

'I don't know. I don't put a mark on my pipe cleaners.'

'Oh well,' said Poirot. 'The pipe cleaner is not important. There are a lot of reasons why it could have been there.'

'Oh!' Arbuthnot looked surprised.

'I wished to see you about something else. Mademoiselle Debenham. She is a most suspicious person.'

'That's not true,' said the Colonel angrily. 'You have no evidence against her.'

'What about this – Mademoiselle Debenham was governess in the Armstrong <u>household</u> at the time of the kidnapping of Daisy Armstrong?'

There was complete silence.

Poirot nodded gently.

'If Mademoiselle Debenham is innocent, why did she hide that fact?'

Colonel Arbuthnot's face looked as though it were cut out of wood.

Poirot called one of the waiters.

'Ask the English lady if she will please come here.'

◆ ◆ ◆

Mary Debenham entered the restaurant carriage, looking confident and proud. At that moment she was beautiful.

'You wished to see me?'

'Yes – to ask you, Mademoiselle, why you lied to us. At the time of the Armstrong kidnapping you were living in the Armstrong family house. Yet you told me you had never been to America.'

Poirot saw she looked worried, but then calm again.

'Yes, I lied.'

'Why, Mademoiselle?'

'I'm sure the reason must be obvious to you,' she said in a calm voice. 'I need to work.'

'You mean…?'

She looked into his face.

'How much do you know, Monsieur Poirot, about how difficult it is to get good employment? Do you think that any respectable Englishwoman would want to employ a governess who had been connected with a murder case?'

And suddenly she laid her face on her arms and started crying as though her heart would break.

The Colonel jumped up and stood beside her, looking embarrassed. 'I – look—'

He looked angrily at Poirot.

'I'll break every bone in your body!'

He turned back to the girl. 'Mary – please—'

She jumped up.

'It's nothing. I'm all right. Oh, how stupid of me!' She hurried out.

Arbuthnot turned once more to Poirot.

'Miss Debenham's not involved with this crime – she's not involved at all, do you hear?'

He walked out.

'I like to see an angry Englishman,' said Poirot. 'They are very amusing.'

But Bouc was not interested in angry Englishmen. He was full of respect for his friend. 'My dear friend,' he cried. 'You are wonderful!'

'It is unbelievable how you think of these things,' said Dr Constantine.

'Oh, Countess Andrenyi almost told me about Miss Debenham.'

'Really?'

'You remember I asked her about her governess?'

'Yes, but the Countess Andrenyi described a completely different person.'

'Yes, indeed. The opposite of Miss Debenham. But then she had to quickly think of a name. She said Miss Freebody, you remember.'

'Yes?'

'Well, there is a shop in London that was called, until recently, Debenham and Freebody. The name Debenham was in her head, so the Countess reaches for another name quickly, and the first that comes is Freebody. Of course I understood immediately.'

'Well,' said Bouc. 'Yet another lie. Why? Does everybody on this train tell lies?'

'That,' said Poirot, 'is what we are about to find out.'

CHAPTER 16

'Nothing would surprise me now,' said Bouc. 'Nothing! Even if it was proved that everybody in the train had been in the Armstrong household.'

'That is a very interesting idea,' said Poirot.

Poriot had asked the waiter to get Antonio Foscarelli. When he brought Foscarelli in, the big Italian had the look of an animal that had been caught.

'I have nothing to tell you – nothing!' He hit the table hard with his hand.

'You do have something more to tell us,' said Poirot. 'The truth!'

'The truth? You talk like the American police. "<u>Come clean</u>," that is what they say—'

'Ah! So you have had experience of the New York police?'

'No, never. They couldn't prove a thing.'

Poirot said quietly:

'That was in the Armstrong case, was it not? You were the <u>chauffeur</u>?'

Foscarelli became very quiet. He was like a balloon that had burst.

'Why did you lie this morning?'

'I had nothing to do with this crime. I never left my compartment. You cannot prove anything against me.'

'All right. You can go,' Poirot said.

But Foscarelli stayed, now even more anxious.

'You know that it wasn't me – that I had nothing to do with it?'

'I said you could go.'

'You're lying. You're going to blame me. All because of a pig of a man who should have gone to the electric chair[9]! Why, that little one – Tonio, she called me. The whole household loved her! Ah, the beautiful little one.'

Tears came into his eyes. He turned suddenly and walked out of the restaurant carriage.

Poirot called to the waiter, who came running.

'From number 10 – the Swedish lady.'

'Of course, Monsieur.'

'Another?' cried Bouc. 'Ah, no – it isn't possible.'

Greta Ohlsson was brought in, crying. She sat down in the seat facing Poirot.

'Do not be upset, Mademoiselle.' Poirot put a friendly hand on her shoulder. 'Just tell us the truth, that is all. You were the nurse in charge of Daisy Armstrong?'

'It's true,' cried the unhappy woman. 'Oh, she was an angel. I was wrong not to tell you the truth. But I was afraid. I felt so happy when I knew that horrible man was dead…'

She cried more and more.

'Don't worry – I will ask you no more questions. It is enough that you have told the truth.'

Greta Ohlsson stood up and made her way towards the door, walking into a man coming in.

It was the valet, Masterman. He came straight to Poirot.

'I thought it best to come at once, sir, and tell you the truth. I worked for Colonel Armstrong in the war, and afterwards I became his valet in New York. It was very wrong of me to hide that fact, sir. But I hope you are not suspecting Tonio in any way. Old Tonio, sir, would not hurt anyone. And I can promise he never left the compartment last night.'

Poirot looked at him but said nothing.

Masterman bowed and left the restaurant carriage.

'This,' said Dr Constantine, 'is all very unlikely.'

'I agree,' said Bouc. 'What next? Or, should I say, who next?'

'I can answer that,' said Poirot. 'Here comes our American detective, Monsieur Hardman.'

'Is he coming to tell us he's done something wrong too?'

Before Poirot could reply, the American had reached their table. He looked hard at them.

'What's going on here? It seems crazy to me.'

Poirot smiled at him.

'Are you sure, Monsieur Hardman, that you were not the person who looked after the garden at the Armstrong home?'

'They didn't have a garden,' replied Hardman. 'I never had any connection with the Armstrong house – but I'm beginning to believe I'm the only one on this train who didn't! It's crazy. They can't all be involved; but I have no idea which one is guilty. Do you know who killed Ratchett?'

Poirot nodded.

'Oh, yes. I have known for some time. If you don't mind, Monsieur Hardman, would you please bring everyone here?'

Chapter 17

The passengers came all together into the restaurant carriage and sat down. They all had the same worried look.

The conductor stood in the doorway. 'Do you mind if I stay, Monsieur?'

'Not at all, Michel.'

Poirot stood up.

'Ladies and gentlemen, we are here to solve the murder of Samuel Ratchett – whose real name was Cassetti. There are two possible solutions to the crime. I shall tell you both, and I shall ask Monsieur Bouc and Dr Constantine to judge which is the right one.

'The evidence of Monsieur Hardman, who is a member of a New York detective agency, shows that the murderer is among those people who are in the Istanbul–Calais carriage.

'But here is another very simple idea. Monsieur Ratchett had an enemy. He told Monsieur Hardman what he looked like, and that he thought this enemy would try to kill him on the second night out from Istanbul.

'Now imagine that, as Monsieur Ratchett expected, this enemy joined the train at *Belgrade, or possibly at Vincovci*. He wore a conductor's uniform over his ordinary clothes and had a key so he was able to get into Monsieur Ratchett's compartment. Monsieur Ratchett was drugged by a drink to help him sleep. This man stabbed him and left the compartment through the door connecting with Madame Hubbard's compartment—'

'That's right,' interrupted Mrs Hubbard.

'He put his knife into Madame Hubbard's wash-bag – and lost a button from his uniform. He went out and along the corridor. He put the uniform into a suitcase in an empty compartment and left the train the way he had entered – the door near the restaurant carriage.'

Everybody looked shocked.

'What about that watch?' demanded Hardman.

'Well, *Monsieur Ratchett hadn't changed the time on his watch* when we came over the border from Eastern Europe. His watch still showed Eastern European time, which is one hour *ahead* of Central European time. It was a quarter past *twelve* when Monsieur Ratchett was stabbed – not a quarter past one.'

'But that's crazy,' cried Bouc. 'The murderer spoke from the compartment at twenty-three minutes to one!'

'Perhaps he didn't. Maybe it was somebody who had gone in to speak to Ratchett and found him dead. He rang the bell to call the conductor, then he became afraid that people might think he was the murderer. So he spoke <u>pretending</u> to be Ratchett.'

'Yes, it's possible,' Bouc said, but he didn't sound like he believed it.

'Well, do you think I forgot to change the time on my watch too?' asked Mrs Hubbard.

Poirot looked at her.

'No, Madame. I think you heard the man pass through your compartment – but you were sleeping. Later you had a nightmare about a man being in your compartment and woke up suddenly and rang for the conductor.'

'Well, that's possible,' admitted Mrs Hubbard.

Princess Dragomiroff was looking very hard at Poirot.

'How do you explain the evidence of my maid, Monsieur?'

'It's very simple, Madame. Your maid knew the handkerchief I showed her was yours. She did see the man – but earlier – while the train was at Vincovci station. She told me she had seen him later with the idea of giving you an <u>alibi</u>.'

The princess bowed her head.

'You have thought of everything, Monsieur. You have my respect.'

There was a silence. Then everyone jumped as Dr Constantine hit the table with his hand.

'No!' he said. 'No! There are many things wrong with that story – Monsieur Poirot must know that.'

Poirot glanced at him in a curious way.

'I see,' he said, 'that I shall have to give my second solution. But do not forget this one. You may agree with it later.'

He turned again to face the others.

'When I had heard all the evidence, I shut my eyes and began to *think*. And certain points seemed very important. The first was something said by Monsieur Bouc on the first day after leaving Istanbul – that the group on the train was interesting because everyone was so different; it was a mix of all levels of society and nationalities.

'I agreed with him, and tried to imagine if such a mix of people was likely to come together in any other way. And my answer was – only in America. In America there might be a household made up of just such a mix – an Italian chauffeur, an English governess, a Swedish nurse, a French lady's maid and so on. That made me think about each person in the Armstrong house.

'I also examined each person's evidence with some strange results. I had described to Monsieur MacQueen the finding of a note about the Armstrong case. He said, "But—" and then went on, "I mean – that was very careless of him."

'I could feel that was not what he had started to say. *Maybe what he had meant to say was, "But that was burned!"* So if *MacQueen knew of the note and that it was burned* – that meant he was either the murderer or he had helped with the murder.

'Then the valet said his employer took a drink to help him sleep. But *why would Ratchett take a drink like that last night?* Ratchett had a gun under his pillow – he intended to protect himself. No, he must have been drugged. If that was true, MacQueen or the valet must have done it.

'Now we come to Monsieur Hardman. The method he used to protect Monsieur Ratchett was useless. The only way to guard Ratchett properly was to stay the night in his compartment. The only thing his evidence *did* show clearly was that no one *in any other part of the train could have murdered Ratchett.* That seemed strange.

'Moving on, you probably have all heard by now of the conversation I heard between Mademoiselle Debenham and Colonel Arbuthnot. The Colonel called her *Mary* and clearly they knew each other well. But the Colonel said he had met her only a few days before. So Colonel Arbuthnot and Mademoiselle Debenham were *pretending* to be strangers.

'Next we have Madame Hubbard, who told us that when she was lying in bed she was unable to see if the door between the carriages was locked. So she asked Mademoiselle Ohlsson to look for her. That would be true if she was in compartment 2, or 4, or any <u>even</u> number – where the bolt is directly under the handle of the door. In the numbers that are not even, such as compartment number 3, the bolt is *above* the handle and the wash-bag could not hide it. So Madame Hubbard was not telling the truth.

'And here let me say something about *times*. The really interesting point about the damaged watch was the place where it was found – in Ratchett's pyjama pocket, an uncomfortable and unlikely place to keep a watch. I felt sure, therefore, that the watch was false. It had been damaged and put in his pocket afterwards. So the crime did not happen at 1.15 am.

'Did it, then, take place earlier? At 12.37 am when a loud cry woke me? But if Ratchett were drugged *he could not cry out.*

'I remembered that MacQueen had told me, not once but twice, that Ratchett could not speak French. I decided that the cry at 12.37 am was like a part of a play, acted just for me! They thought I *would* know the watch business was false. Then I would think that, as Ratchett spoke no French, the voice I heard at 12.37 am could not be his. And so Ratchett must already be dead.

'But in fact I think Ratchett was killed very nearly at two o'clock, the latest hour the doctor gave us as possible.

'Now, on to who killed him...'

He paused. Everyone was looking at him. There was complete silence.

He continued slowly:

'I was particularly worried about the problem of proving a case against any one person on the train. The way that everyone's alibi came from an "unlikely" person was very strange. For example, Monsieur MacQueen and Colonel Arbuthnot provided alibis for each other – two people most unlikely to have met before. The same happened with the English valet and the Italian, with the Swedish lady and the English girl. I said to myself, "This is extraordinary – they cannot *all* be involved!"

'And then, Messieurs, I understood. They *were* all involved. It was impossible that so many people connected with the Armstrong case were travelling by the same train by chance. The murder was planned. I remembered what Colonel Arbuthnot had said about trial by jury. A jury is twelve people – there were twelve passengers – Ratchett was stabbed twelve times. The extraordinary crowd travelling in the Istanbul–Calais coach was explained.

'Ratchett was never punished for his crime in America. There was no doubt that he was guilty. I thought of twelve people who had decided to become their own jury. They had decided Ratchett must die and that they would kill him. And immediately the whole case became beautifully clear.

'It was arranged that if any one person should be suspected, the evidence of one or more of the others would give them an alibi. Hardman's evidence was necessary in case some outside person was suspected and was unable to provide an alibi. Every detail was worked out before, so that everything I learned made the solution more difficult.

'Did this solution explain everything? Yes, it did. The wounds – each one was made by a different person. The false letters were shown as evidence. MacQueen destroyed the real letters telling Ratchett he would die because of Daisy Armstrong. Then Hardman's story of being employed by Ratchett – that was a lie. The *"small dark-haired man with a voice like a woman's"* did not exist.

'The knife could be used by everyone – strong or weak – and made no noise. I think that each person, one after another, entered Ratchett's dark compartment through Madame Hubbard's – and struck! Nobody would ever know which blow killed him.

'The final letter, which Ratchett had probably found on his pillow, was burned. With no connection to the Armstrong case, there would be no reason for suspecting any of the passengers on the train. People would think the murder was done by someone from outside. The *"small dark-haired man with the voice like a woman's"* would actually have been seen by one or more of the passengers leaving the train at Brod.

'That part of the plan was impossible because of the snow, which meant that the passengers would now be suspected. But alibis for all of them were already planned. The only extra thing to be done was to make things even more complicated. Two "clues" were dropped in the dead man's compartment – one incriminating Colonel Arbuthnot (who had the strongest alibi and whose connection with the Armstrong family was the hardest to prove). The second clue, the handkerchief, incriminated Princess Dragomiroff, who by her position in society, her weak body and the alibi given her by her maid and the conductor, was completely safe. To make everything more complicated, a false clue appeared – the woman in the red dressing-gown. She did not exist, but cleverly I was woken and made to see 'her' in the corridor, meaning that I am one of the people to say that she is real.

'It was, I think, someone with a sense of humour who later put the dressing-gown in my suitcase...

'When MacQueen learned that the burned letter had not been completely destroyed by the fire, the position of Countess Andrenyi became dangerous. Her husband immediately decided to change the passport.

'There was one more point. The conductor himself must have been part of the plan. But if so, that gave us thirteen people, not twelve. Which one was innocent?

'I had a strange idea. The person who had taken no part in the crime was the person who would be the most likely to do so. Countess Andrenyi. Her husband promised me that his wife never left her compartment that night. I decided that Count Andrenyi had taken his wife's place.

'If that was correct, then how was Pierre Michel part of the Armstrong case? Then I remembered the dead maid who was French. Perhaps she had been Pierre Michel's daughter? That would explain everything – it would also explain the place chosen for the crime. Were there any others whose part in the drama was not clear? Colonel Arbuthnot, I decided, was a friend of Armstrong; they had probably been through the war together.

'Then there was Hardman. He seemed quite definitely not to belong to the Armstrong household. I imagined that perhaps he had been in love with the French girl. I spoke to him about French and Belgian women – and I saw what I was looking for. Sudden tears came to his eyes, which he pretended were because the snow was so bright. So I was right.

'There is still Madame Hubbard. Now Madame Hubbard, let me say, played the most important part in the drama. Because her compartment was next to Ratchett's, people were more likely to suspect her than anyone else. She could not have an alibi. To play the part she played – a rather silly American mother – a professional actor was needed. But there *was* a professional actor connected with the Armstrong family – Mrs Armstrong's mother – Linda Arden…'

In a soft voice, completely different from the one she had used during the journey, Mrs Hubbard said:

'That mistake about the wash-bag was silly. It shows you should always practise everything properly. We tried it on the journey to Istanbul – in an even number compartment. I never thought about the bolts being in different places.'

She moved a little and looked straight at Poirot.

'You know everything, Monsieur Poirot. You're a very wonderful man. But even you can't imagine what it was like – that awful day in New York. I was mad with the terrible shock of Daisy's death – so was the whole household – and Colonel Arbuthnot was there, too. He was John Armstrong's best friend.'

'He saved my life in the war,' said Arbuthnot.

Mrs Hubbard – Linda Arden – continued: 'Perhaps we really were mad, I don't know. But we decided that the death which Cassetti had escaped had to take place. In the end we decided on this way. It was the chauffeur, Antonio, who suggested it. Mary worked out all the details later with Hector MacQueen. He'd always thought Sonia – my daughter – was wonderful, and it was he who explained to us how Cassetti's money had saved him.

'It took a long time to get our plan ready. Hardman found out where Ratchett was, then we had to get Masterman and Hector into his employment. After that, we spoke with Susanne's father

– she was his only child so he was very willing to be our twelfth person.

'We knew from Hector that Ratchett would be coming back from the east by the Orient Express. With Pierre Michel working on that train, we could not miss this excellent opportunity.

'My daughter's husband had to know, of course, and he insisted on coming with her. We meant to have every compartment in the Istanbul-Calais carriage, but unfortunately there was one that was kept for a director of the company – Mr Bouc. Mr Harris, of course, did not exist. It would have been difficult to have a stranger in Hector's compartment. And then, at the last minute, *you* came...'

She stopped.

'Well,' she said. 'You know everything now, Monsieur Poirot. Can't you blame me and only me? I would have happily stabbed that man twelve times. He was responsible for my daughter's death and her child's, and that of the baby who might be alive and happy now. But it was more than that – we knew there had been other children before Daisy – there might be others in the future...'

Her voice was wonderful – that strong voice that had brought pleasure to many New York theatre audiences.

Poirot looked at his friend.

'You are a director of the company, Monsieur Bouc,' he said, 'What do you say?'

Bouc coughed.

'In my opinion, Monsieur Poirot,' he said, 'the first explanation you suggested was the correct one. I suggest that is the solution we offer the police when they arrive. Do you agree, Doctor?'

'Certainly, I agree,' said Dr Constantine.

'Then,' said Poirot, 'my part in the case... is over.'

✦ Character list ✦

Hercule Poirot: famous Belgian private detective, living in London

Monsieur Bouc: director of the Compagnie Internationale des Wagons Lits

Dr Constantine: Greek doctor travelling on the Simplon Orient Express

Miss Mary Debenham: English governess working for a family in Baghdad

Colonel Arbuthnot: on holiday from the British Army in India

Mrs Hubbard: American lady who never stops talking

Princess Natalia Dragomiroff: elderly and very rich Russian princess

Samuel Ratchett: rich American businessman

Hector MacQueen: young American secretary to Mr Ratchett

Count Rudolph Andrenyi: working at the Hungarian Embassy in Istanbul

Countess Elena Andrenyi: beautiful young wife of Count Andrenyi

Cyrus Hardman: American salesman, travelling from Istanbul to Paris

Antonio Foscarelli: Italian car salesman who has become a US citizen

Greta Ohlsson: Swedish nurse

Hildegarde Schmidt: German maid to Princess Dragomiroff

Edward Masterman: English valet to Samuel Ratchett

Pierre Michel: French conductor on the Orient Express

The Istanbul–Calais carriage of the Simplon Orient Express

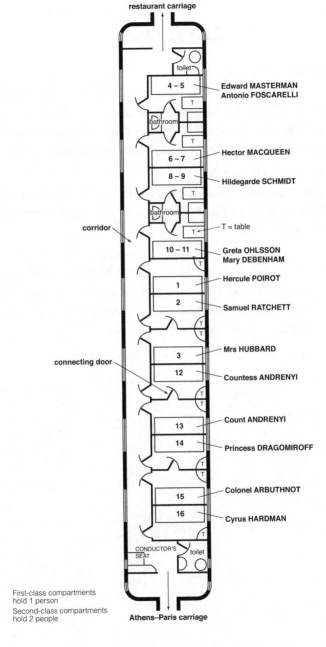

restaurant carriage

toilet

4 – 5 — Edward MASTERMAN
Antonio FOSCARELLI

T

bathroom

T

6 – 7 — Hector MACQUEEN

8 – 9 — Hildegarde SCHMIDT

T

bathroom

corridor

T — T = table

10 – 11 — Greta OHLSSON
Mary DEBENHAM

T

1 — Hercule POIROT

2 — Samuel RATCHETT

T
T

connecting door

3 — Mrs HUBBARD

12 — Countess ANDRENYI

T
T

13 — Count ANDRENYI

14 — Princess DRAGOMIROFF

T
T

15 — Colonel ARBUTHNOT

16 — Cyrus HARDMAN

T

CONDUCTOR'S
SEAT   toilet

First-class compartments
hold 1 person
Second-class compartments
hold 2 people

Athens–Paris carriage

◆ Cultural notes ◆

1. The Taurus Express
The Taurus Express was a luxury passenger train service created in 1930 by the Compagnie Internationale des Wagons-Lits – the International Company for Sleeping Carriages. In the past, it went overnight from Istanbul to Baghdad, but today it goes between Eskişehir and Adana in Turkey.

2. The Simplon Orient Express
The Orient Express is a luxury passenger train service created in 1883 by the Compagnie Internationale des Wagons-Lits. The first trains went from Paris to Istanbul.

In 1919 the Simplon Orient Express service began. This service, which ran at the same time as the traditional Orient Express, had a more southern route, through Milan and Venice. It went through the Simplon Tunnel, one of the longest railway tunnels in the world, which connects Switzerland and Italy through the Alps (see map).

A version of the Simplon Orient Express still runs today.

Route of the Simplon Orient Express

3. Balzac
Honoré de Balzac (1799–1850) was a French writer of novels and plays. He had a great talent for describing people from different levels of society in detail.

4. Persia
Modern-day Iran.

5. District Attorney
In the United States, a lawyer who works for a city or area. He or she tries to prove that someone believed to have carried out a crime is guilty. In this story, the district attorney's job was to prove that Cassetti was guilty.

6. Diplomatic passport
A passport held by someone with an important job in a foreign Embassy. It gives that person special benefits and advantages when travelling.

7. Trial by jury
A method of deciding by law if someone is guilty of a crime in serious criminal cases. A judge and twelve members of the public (the jury) listen to the evidence. The jury then decide if the person is guilty or innocent. The 'trial by jury' method is used in many countries and is generally thought to be very fair.

8. Citizen
Someone who is a citizen of a country is accepted by law as belonging to that country.

9. The electric chair
Often known as 'the chair', this is a method of killing criminals, used especially in the United States. The person is tied to a special chair and electricity is passed through it.

◆ GLOSSARY ◆

alibi COUNTABLE NOUN
If you have an **alibi**, you can prove that you were somewhere else when a crime took place.

blow COUNTABLE NOUN
If someone receives a **blow**, they are hit by someone or something.

bolt COUNTABLE NOUN
A **bolt** on a door or window is a metal bar that you slide across to fasten it.
TRANSITIVE VERB
If you **bolt** a door or window, you slide the bolt across to fasten it.

bow INTRANSITIVE VERB
When you **bow** to someone, you briefly bend your body towards them as a formal way of greeting them.

carelessly ADVERB
If someone does or says something **carelessly**, they do or say it without paying very much attention.

carriage COUNTABLE NOUN
A **carriage** is one of the separate sections of a train that carries passengers.

case COUNTABLE NOUN
A **case** is a crime that the police are working on.

chauffeur COUNTABLE NOUN
A **chauffeur** is a person whose job is to drive and look after another person's car.

class
First-**class** accommodation is the best and most expensive accommodation on a train or ship. Second-**class** accommodation on a train or ship is cheaper and less comfortable than first-class.

clue COUNTABLE NOUN
A **clue** to a problem or mystery is something that helps you find the answer.

colonel COUNTABLE NOUN
A **colonel** is a senior person in the army, navy or air force.

come clean PHRASE
If you **come clean** about something that you have been keeping secret, you admit it.

compartment COUNTABLE NOUN
A **compartment** is a small room where people sit, and sometimes sleep, in a train carriage.

conductor COUNTABLE NOUN
On a train, a **conductor** is a person whose job is to travel on the train in order to help passengers and check tickets.

Count, Countess TITLE NOUN
A **Count** and a **Countess** are
members of a high social group.

dressing-gown COUNTABLE NOUN
A **dressing-gown** is a loose coat
worn over pyjamas or other
night clothes.

drug TRANSITIVE VERB
If you **drug** a person, you give
them a pill or a drink in order
to make them sleepy.

eagerly ADVERB
If you say something **eagerly**,
you say it like you very much
want it to happen.

embroidered ADJECTIVE
If a piece of cloth is
embroidered, a design is sewn
into it.

even number COUNTABLE NOUN
An **even number** can be divided
exactly by the number two.

evidence UNCOUNTABLE NOUN
Evidence is information which
is used to prove that something
is true.

examine TRANSITIVE VERB
If you **examine** something,
you look at it carefully.

ferret COUNTABLE NOUN
A **ferret** is a small animal with
a long thin body which is used for
hunting rabbits and rats.

fingerprint COUNTABLE NOUN
Your **fingerprints** are the marks
made by your fingers when you
touch something.

godmother COUNTABLE NOUN
If a woman is the **godmother**
of a younger person, she
promises to help bring them
up as a Christian.

governess COUNTABLE NOUN
A **governess** is a woman who
lives with a family and teaches
their children.

grease UNCOUNTABLE NOUN
Grease is animal fat which
comes from cooking meat.

guilty ADJECTIVE
If someone is **guilty** of
committing a crime, they have
committed a crime.

handle COUNTABLE NOUN
A **handle** is a small object that
is attached to a door and is used
for opening and closing it.

household COUNTABLE NOUN
A **household** is all the people
in a family, and the people who
work for them, who live together
in a house.

incriminate TRANSITIVE VERB
If something **incriminates** you,
it suggests that you are the
person who has done a crime.

innocent ADJECTIVE
If someone is **innocent**, they did not do a crime which other people said they did.

kidnap TRANSITIVE VERB
To **kidnap** someone is to take them away, and usually to keep them somewhere and demand something from their family to give them back.

kidnapping VARIABLE NOUN
Kidnapping is when someone is kidnapped.

law SINGULAR NOUN
The **law** is a system of rules that a society or government develops in order to deal with crime.

lieutenant COUNTABLE NOUN
A **lieutenant** is a junior person in the army, navy, or air force.

little grey cells PHRASE
You can talk about your brains as **little grey cells**.

maid COUNTABLE NOUN
A **maid** is a woman who works for a person or family.

mark COUNTABLE NOUN
If something makes a **mark** on something, a small area of that thing is damaged.

match COUNTABLE NOUN
A **match** is a small wooden stick that produces a flame when you strike one end against something rough.

miracle COUNTABLE NOUN
A **miracle** is an event that cannot be explained by science or nature.

nod INTRANSITIVE VERB
If you **nod**, you move your head down and up to show that you understand or like something, or that you agree with it.

pipe cleaner COUNTABLE NOUN
A **pipe cleaner** is a short piece of wire covered with a soft material.

pretend TRANSITIVE VERB
If you **pretend** that something is true, you try to make people believe that it is true, although it is not.

pyjamas PLURAL NOUN
A pair of **pyjamas** consists of loose trousers and a loose jacket that are worn in bed.

respectable ADJECTIVE
Someone who is **respectable** is liked and respected by other people.

responsible for ADJECTIVE
If you are **responsible for** something bad that has happened, it is your fault.

revenge UNCOUNTABLE NOUN
Revenge involves hurting someone who has hurt you.

search COUNTABLE NOUN
A **search** is an attempt to find something by looking for it carefully.
TRANSITIVE VERB
If you **search** a place, you look carefully for someone or something there.

shake one's head PHRASE
If you **shake your head**, you move it from side to side in order to say 'no'.

sigh INTRANSITIVE VERB
When you **sigh**, you let out a deep breath.

stab TRANSITIVE VERB
If someone **stabs** another person, they push a knife into their body.

suspect COUNTABLE NOUN
A **suspect** is a person who the police think may be guilty of a crime.
TRANSITIVE VERB
If you say that you **suspect** that something is true, you mean that you believe that it is probably true, but you want to make it sound less strong or direct.

suspicious ADJECTIVE
If someone or something is **suspicious**, there is something about them which makes you think that they are involved in a crime.

thoughtfully ADVERB
If do or say something **thoughtfully**, you do or say it in a quiet and serious way because you are thinking.

threaten VERB
If someone **threatens** to do something unpleasant to you, they say that they will do something unpleasant to you, especially if you do not do what they want.

valet COUNTABLE NOUN
A **valet** is a man who works for a person or family.

victim COUNTABLE NOUN
A **victim** is someone who has been hurt or killed by someone or something.

violent ADJECTIVE
If someone does something which is **violent**, they hurt or kill other people, sometimes using something like a gun or a knife.

wound COUNTABLE NOUN
A **wound** is when part of your body has been hurt, especially when it is a cut or hole caused by something like a gun or a knife.